The Gold
of Thrace

Also by Aileen G. Baron

A Fly Has a Hundred Eyes
The Torch of Tangier

The Gold of Thrace

Aileen G. Baron

Poisoned Pen Press

Copyright © 2007 by Aileen G. Baron

First U. S. Edition 2007

10 9 8 7 6 5 4 3 2 1

Library of Congress Catalog Card Number: 2006940931

ISBN: 978-1-59058-430-9 Hardcover

Poisoned Pen Press
6962 E. First Ave., Ste. 103
Scottsdale, AZ 85251
www.poisonedpenpress.com
info@poisonedpenpress.com

Printed in the United States of America

To Carrie and Henry Garsson. Thank you.

Acknowledgments

I would like to thank Dr. Engin Özgen, of Hacettepe University, Ankara, and former Director of Antiquities and Heritage of Turkey, for suggesting that I write a mystery about the antiquities trade, and for leading me on an exhaustive tour of Ephesus and other Turkish sites.

My thanks, as always, go to Linda McFadden, Sally Scalzo, and Cathy De Mayo for advice on the first drafts of this book, to Dr. David M. Baron for his expertise and suggestions, and to James S. Baron for enthusiastic ideas for some of the scenes and settings.

I would also like to thank Thomas Shreves of the Getty Conservation Institute for sending me extensive literature on dating gold artifacts, and Ozgun Tumer of the Yorba Linda Library for his advice on Turkish names and places.

And of course, my special thanks go to Barbara Peters, the world's greatest editor, to publisher Rob Rosenwald, and to Jessica Tribble, Marilyn Pizzo and the rest of the staff at Poisoned Pen Press for a superb job well done.

Chapter One

Ephesus, Turkey, August 6, 1990

"I saw it all," the American woman was saying.

She was one of the tourists off the cruise ship. The American woman wore a Greek fisherman's hat, a T-shirt emblazoned with gilt and dark blue anchors, sandals bedecked with plastic flowers, and she was trembling.

She had come to see Ephesus, banking and trading center of the east Mediterranean in Roman times; capital and principal port of the province of Asia; the richest city in the Roman Empire; city of Artemis, the famous Diana of Ephesus, who was barnacled with mammaries from her neck to her waist.

Instead, the American stood next to the body of a man who lay on the mosaic walkway on the Street of the Curetes, where once priests of the beautiful Artemis paraded to the sounds of flutes, drums and cymbals, clashing their swords against their shields, banging their tambourines, flagellating themselves with whips until they bled, whirling and dancing, castrating and mutilating themselves to celebrate the birth of Artemis.

"What did you see?" the detective asked the American woman, his pencil poised over a notebook.

Police cars with flashing lights stood nose to nose in the parking lot amid tour buses.

Policemen herded them all—the Frenchmen with red berets and bandanas behind a guide flourishing a red banner, the Germans with yellow golf caps and shoulder bags and their guide with her yellow pennant—past empty columns over marble streets. They passed the Library of Celsus, designed by the great architect Vitruvius, they passed Trajan's fountain, they passed the Temple of Hadrian, and jostled for space on their way to the buses to take them back to Izmir, to Kusadasi, to Selçuk, to the cruise ships that lay offshore.

"What did you see?" the policeman asked the American woman again.

"He came out of nowhere," the American woman said. "He had something shiny in his hand, a knife. It glinted in the sun."

A few stragglers, camcorders on their shoulders, broke from the crowd and started toward them. A gaggle of Americans emerged, laughing, from the Roman latrine where they had been sitting on the concrete toilets, just as the pilgrims who came for the festival of Artemis had done long ago, just as Ephesians who paused in their morning ablutions to sit for a while and catch up on the latest gossip.

The policemen drove them all back into the throng and it milled past the theater where bulls and manhood were sacrificed for the glory of Artemis, where terrible myths were acted out, where the bulls were slaughtered in sacrifice and the goddess festooned with their testes and dripped with blood, where the Ephesians attacked St. Paul, where they stoned him shouting, "Great is the Artemis of the Ephesians."

The American woman remembered for a moment that they weren't mammaries; they were bull's testicles.

She sighed and rubbed her arms as if she were cold. "He lunged. He had a knife."

"Go on," the detective said, his pen still hovering over the pad.

Policemen steered the swarms of tourists into the parking lot next to the road from the ancient harbor that was once lined with shops and grand public buildings, where visitors would stroll in the shade of a columned portico anticipating the spectacle they came so far to see, stopping at food and wine merchants, stopping at shops where they bought silver statuettes of the beautiful Diana of Ephesus, anticipating the delicious tingle of horror as the attendants of the goddess and her neophytes mutilated themselves in her honor.

"Please," the detective said.

She pointed to the body on the ground. "He dropped silent as a stone."

The American woman closed her eyes and saw him fall again, his blood seeping into the ground where the curetes bled. She began to shudder. Her husband put his arm over her shoulder and she leaned on him.

"What did he look like?" the detective asked.

"The man with the knife?" her husband said. "Thickset, with curly gray hair. He looked like he was sneering."

"Which way did he go?" the detective asked.

"That way," the American woman said and pointed vaguely in the direction of the parking lot.

The detective wrote that in his notebook.

"That way," her husband said and pointed toward Selçuk, toward the Basilica of Saint John on the hill.

The detective wrote that, too, in his notebook. He dispatched two policemen, one to the parking lot, the other to the Basilica of Saint John, and waited to hear from the man who was hurrying down from the Roman houses on the slope.

"Dr. Kosay?" the detective called.

Dr. Kosay was bald, with earnest hazel eyes and a Turkish moustache. He nodded as he ran down the hill. "Atalay Kosay," the man said between puffs of breath. "I could see some of what happened from up above."

The detective turned to a new page in his notebook. "What did you see?"

Kosay looked at the body on the pavement and his face went pale.

"You know him?"

"He was my student. His name is Binali Gul."

"He was working with you here at Ephesus?"

Kosay shook his head. "Not here. He's from the University at Izmir. He was digging at Tepe Hazarken."

"What was he doing here?"

"He came to tell me something. He said it was important."

"What was it?"

"I don't know."

"What did you see?" the detective asked again.

"A thickset man with curly gray hair stabbed Binali. Then he ran off toward the Kusadasi road."

The detective wrote in his notebook that a thickset man with curly gray hair stabbed Binali Gul and ran off in three directions, then signaled for a third policeman.

"We will have to close down Ephesus for a few hours," the policeman told Kosay as sirens began to wail in the museum half a kilometer away.

"Certainly," Kosay said.

The detective spread his hands as if to ask a question and looked at Kosay, but Kosay was watching the woman running toward them from the museum.

"They broke into a case," she told Kosay between gasps of breath. "They stole the golden Kybele."

"The Kybele?" Kosay said. "They stole the Kybele?"

The policeman turned to a new page in his notebook. "Did you see who did it?" he asked the woman.

She shook her head. "Just heard the alarm. By the time I reached the case, the room was empty, the Kybele was gone."

"She wasn't from Ephesus," Kosay said. "The Kybele was on loan, entrusted to me."

"What is a Kybele?" the American woman asked.

"The Goddess," Kosay said. "The Mother Goddess, the oldest, the greatest goddess. She is Anatolia."

Chapter Two

Kilis, Turkey, August 7, 1990

Tamar watched impatiently as the man from Ankara spilled bits of pottery from plastic bags onto a table set up in the shade of an umbrella, watched him sort through the sherds quickly, his hand moving them to the right or left.

They had been at it all morning, the three of them—Tamar Saticoy and Orman Çelibi, co-directors of the excavations at Tepe Hazarfen, and Mustafa Yeğin, the man with intense eyes and flowing moustache from the Department of Antiquities at Ankara.

The death of Binali hung over them like a cloud.

Three days ago Tamar had been supervising the excavation of a Roman house on the far side of Tepe Hazarfen, the archaeological site that loomed behind the village of Hazarfen, when she spotted the *tessera*, a small mosaic tile of pale marble no more than a quarter of an inch on each side. She held it in her hand, thrilled with the excitement of discovery, with pleasurable anticipation of uncovering the mosaic that lay below the dusty field where she stood.

That was the beginning for Tamar. Nothing would be the same after that. Finding it affected everything.

She had stopped her students, some with pickaxes in mid-swing, told them to go slower, to watch for a mosaic floor just below the surface and showed them how to remove the overburden inside the thin interior wall of the room with a flat-nosed shovel. When they had almost reached the floor, she sent them away, afraid that their carelessness would damage the mosaic.

For two days, with only Binali to help her, she cleared the room, first scraping away the dirt with the side of trowels, then by herself with a whiskbroom and finally with a soft rat-tailed brush, until a pattern emerged.

She didn't fully appreciate what she had found until she wiped it clean with water and the tiles sparkled in the sun. She stood back and caught her breath.

The floor had all the complexity of a superb oriental rug—a twisted guilloche around the edge, clusters of lush ripe fruit at the corners. In the center, surrounded by a design of involuted flowered vines, a medallion was adorned with the striking image of a woman—a sloe-eyed enchantress with the grace of a goddess.

Tamar knelt down and traced along the edge of the medallion with her fingers, along the image of the lady—the magnificent arch of her neck, the soft curvature of her cheek, the elegant rosettes of bronze-gold hair that framed her face.

The mosaic was the work of a master.

The lady's turquoise eyes, half-closed, glanced suggestively to the side and her seductive smile seemed poised to break into beguiling speech.

Why is it, Tamar wondered, we always uncover the best finds the last day of the season? She gave a resigned sigh and turned back to the mosaic, hurrying to finish before the light failed.

When they were ready to leave, Orman helped her cover the floor with a tarp. They weighted the tarp down at the sides with stones to protect the mosaic until the next day and the meeting with Mustafa Yeğin.

They made their way down the hill, to the van parked near the coffeehouse at the entrance to Hazarfen, past the houses and outbuildings of the village below the site, past the mud-brick walls with the tinder for winter fuel already stacked high against them, got into the van and drove off for the dig house in Kilis.

◇◇◇

And now, she waited as Yeğin sorted through the pottery.

Heavy plastic bags filled with artifacts, labeled and ready to be read, lay on the ground. A small collection that she and Orman could take home to the States for analysis was heaped on one side of the table; a larger pile that Yeğin was bringing back to Ankara was stacked near his camp chair.

Tamar and Orman were the only ones from Tepe Hazarfen at the division. Everyone else had gone home.

The other director, Andrew Chatham, had left. He intended to stop in Prague to visit his mother, he said, before returning to the British Museum.

Typical, Tamar thought; Chatham always left the dirty work to others, especially in the field.

Chatham would sit, comfortable under an umbrella, flourishing his sunglasses and his cigarette holder, leaning back in his chair, waiting for the workmen to bring him whole pots from tomb after tomb.

According to the agreement with the Turkish government, archaeologists were required to hire local workmen to help with the excavation. Chatham had appropriated every one of them.

He paid the workmen for the pottery. At first he paid them by the piece until he noticed fresh breaks, he told Tamar and Orman at dinner. He was sure that the workers broke up whole pots from the tombs to get more money for each piece, so he was offering a substantial bonus for whole pots.

After that, pottery seemed to erupt from the tombs. Chatham could hardly keep up with the flow of artifacts, had little time to check the drawings and find-spots. Day after day, hour after hour, he was inundated with ceramics, some with a chip missing here and there, some still encrusted with dirt from the tombs.

At dinner, Chatham would wink at Tamar and Orman and tell them that that was the way to dig, not to get your hands dirty, not to bother with students and supervision and lectures.

"It's a fountain of plenty," he told them. "This cemetery shines like a supernova in the constellation of excavations."

His reputation, he told them, was made.

◇◇◇

Tamar watched Mustafa Yeğin sort another bag of sherds, repack them, tag the bag with a registration number and mark it for Ankara. He seemed tantalizingly slow and careful as he tagged the bags and tied them. He glanced at Tamar with a questioning look as she tapped her foot and drummed her fingers on the table. His face seemed to wear a perpetual frown, incised into his forehead like a scar, and when he spoke the tone was always ponderous, as if he were importing weighty news.

"Impatient for some reason?" he asked.

"The villa. The mosaic floor."

"All in good time." His voice was low and deliberate. "We'll get to Tepe Hazarfen after lunch."

Mustafa came from Istanbul, according to Chatham. He took courses at Cambridge and worked for a while at the British Museum before he returned to Turkey. Chatham had known him in Istanbul, and recommended him for the job at the British Museum.

By midmorning Mustafa had gotten as far as the special finds: metal, inscribed pieces, whole pots and the material from Chatham's cemetery.

He lifted one of the pots from the cemetery, balanced it in his hand, took a loupe from his pocket, squinted through it, his nose wrinkled in concentration, and shook his head. He tossed most of the pottery into the bin marked for the British Museum.

Tamar picked up one and cautiously licked it with her tongue, giving it a rough and ready test. If it was slick, the pottery was probably modern. If her tongue stuck, it was probably in the ground for a long time, interacting with the surrounding soil. Tiny flakes, too small to be seen by the naked eye, would have spalled off and abraded the exterior, leaving the surface irregular.

"Fake?" she asked.

Mustafa nodded. "It seems so. Somewhere in the village of Hazarfen, there is a pottery workshop that manufactures authentic antiquities to order."

In the end, only twelve pots remained on the table.

"Could be the next village over," Tamar said. "There were always visitors. They brought truckloads filled with what they called gifts. Said they came to arrange marriages. They sat in the coffeehouse next to the school and bargained the whole day."

"Why do you work with Chatham?" Mustafa asked.

Tamar pictured Chatham, imperious and immaculate in the shade, with his pencil-thin blond mustache, an ascot arranged at his neck even on the warmest days. "It's his British charm."

"I heard he was born in Hungary."

"Czechoslovakia," Tamar said. "His name was originally Andor Chaloupek. He fled to London after the Russians came in, changed his name to Andrew Chatham, and now he's more British than the queen."

Mustafa shook his head. "And you dig with an idiot like that?"

She laughed. "It's his good looks." Chatham always dressed the part, with his white linen britches, his riding boots, his safari shirt. "He got us the license to dig the site, helped us get financing. His father-in-law has vitamin P and vitamin M."

"Pull and money?" Mustafa asked.

Tamar nodded and laughed.

Orman shook his head. "Don't defend him. He made advances to one of my students. And once he cornered the cook."

Orman's face seemed to be all points with its fine pointed cheekbones, a delicate pointed nose, and a smile that caught at the corners of his eyes.

Mustafa wrapped the pots on the table, tagged and boxed them, taped them shut and labeled them.

"We've finished here." He smiled at Tamar. "Off to Hazarfen."

"At last," she said.

They stopped for a brief lunch in Kilis and reached Hazarfen shortly after one o'clock. The drive, a little over eight kilometers, took fifteen minutes. Orman was driving.

He slowed the van as they came to the end of the paved road.

They brushed the dust of the drive from their clothes and trudged through dry grass, crisp against their soles in the hot summer afternoon.

"The mosaic floor is in a Roman villa," Tamar said to Mustafa. "You'll have to decide whether to preserve it *in situ* or lift it and bring it in to the museum."

"Not much money in our budget."

"We could apply for a grant from the Getty. Or the Volkswagen Foundation."

"Maybe. First let's see it."

She led them over the top of the hill and down the saddle away from the village. "I haven't photographed it yet. We need a photographer with a tower."

Below them, one of the village women, her head covered with a scarf, her dark dress flapping against her ankles in the summer breeze, was laying out wash on the roof of one of the houses. She glanced up at the three of them on the top of the hill and waved. Tamar waved back.

When Tamar first came to Hazarfen three seasons ago, all the villagers were strangers. She had loped through the hamlet and over fallow fields bright with wild tulips and poppies with the trepidation of an outsider. Drawn by the ruins of Greek columns and Roman arches outlined against the bright blue sky on the hill above, she had climbed the narrow alleys between house compounds, skirting the kindling piled against their mud-brick walls, and up to the tel.

The village below her seemed caught in time, the walled farmhouses and courtyards echoing ancient prototypes: wells in the courtyards; farmers repairing flat roofs with clay rollers; low ceilings in ground floor cotes for sheep and goats and outside stairs that led to living quarters above them. All reflected the dusty remnants of long-gone villages, the remains of collapsed houses that she had found in ancient settlements. The whole world was here—the past, the present—vivid and alive with the smells and heat of reality.

That first day of the first season, she had climbed on the roof of a saint's tomb on the top of the hill to scan the ten-by-ten meter squares laid out with surveyors' pins. The villagers had been paid for the use of their fields, paid to work on the tel. The men leaned on their shovels, daring her, watching her, waiting to see what she would do.

Now the people in the village were her friends. She laughed at their children's play; she drank the water from their wells. She sipped coffee with the women in the shade of pistachio trees in their courtyards and carried eggs from their chickens back to the dig house at Kilis.

She would nod and smile when they talked, her knowledge of Turkish too fragmentary to join them in conversation. She knew just enough to say good morning, please, thank you. The women of the village didn't seem to mind. They clasped their arms around her and greeted her with kisses when she arrived in the morning, and waved when she rode back with the others to Kilis at the end of the day.

"The villa is in a *latifundia*," Tamar told Mustafa. "The ancient Roman farming complex of a rich man."

They made their way past the stubs of ancient walls of out-buildings.

"Next season," she said, "I thought I'd dig in the foundry, recover some tools—plowshares, bits of nails and knives, axes, mattocks...."

"If there is a next season."

Tamar turned to look at Mustafa. "What do you mean?"

"Even Chatham's rich father-in-law will have a hard time convincing the Department of Antiquities that he can be trusted."

When the three of them reached the Roman house, Tamar paused to give them time to arrange themselves around the tarp. Orman stood at the right of the mosaic, and Mustafa at the foot where he could have the best view. Carefully, she lifted the stones from around the edges of the tarp, and with a flourish, threw back the covering.

Only dust lay under the tarp.

The mosaic was gone.

Chapter Three

Istanbul, Turkey, August 7, 1990

Something was wrong, but Chatham couldn't put his finger on it. Maybe it was the man with the worn black bag who watched him when he stopped at the kiosk at Sirkeci railroad station to buy a paper. The man stood near the buffet, trying to look like he wasn't paying attention. He had a bulbous nose and glasses, and from this distance it looked like his cheeks were pitted with acne scars.

The kiosk was sold out of the *London Times*. Chatham had to settle for a day-old *Herald Tribune*. He could feel the man with the suitcase watch him as he took the change from his pocket and paid for the paper. When Chatham left the stand, their eyes met. The man turned away.

Nothing was going right today. The hotel in Istanbul woke him late with breakfast, his tea was cold, he was forced to dress and pack and gulp his tea at the same time if he wanted to make the train.

His wife Emma called to tell him about the murder of Binali Gul. He thought about it a minute, then said, "Send flowers."

He was about to hang up when she began to argue again. He had been up half the night ruminating over their last encounter, reliving the anger, the bitterness.

And the long queue at the hotel desk when he checked out, the cold stare from the clerk when his credit card was rejected. Damn Emma.

At the cashier's cage, he pulled out a pen and wrote a check. "I'll miss the train," he mumbled. "You know me. I've been coming here for years."

"Yes, Mr. Chatham."

"Professor Chatham."

"Of course. *Professor*."

No need to be subjected to this indignity.

"Sorry for the inconvenience, professor."

He hurried out to a cab, his bag banging against his leg. The taxi reeked of stale tobacco. Smoke from the driver's cigarette blew back in his face and tiny sparks flew out the open window.

He was unhappy about the route the train would take, through the Balkans. They could blow any day now. Since the dissolution of the Soviet Union a few years ago, the Balkans were trouble. Without Russian support, the only way to make a living was smuggling and stealing from your neighbor.

And any day now, Yugoslavia was going to shatter into ethnic enclaves like splinters of a broken pot. The whole region was being, well, Balkanized. Every village would seek revenge for wounds five hundred years old, and rivers of hatred would flow, ice cold, from every crag and mountain.

Balkanized. That was the word. He laughed out loud, and caught the look the driver gave him in the rear view mirror.

From the train window, Chatham saw the man with the suitcase again, peering into car after car.

And now the man was on the train, flinging open the door of Chatham's compartment. This close, Chatham saw that his ill-fitting suit was brushed to a shine and the suitcase, made of cardboard, had a wide scratch along one side that ran diagonally from one corner to another.

Chatham snapped his paper upright and began reading. Without a word, the man disappeared.

At the border, the train stopped for customs checks at Kapi-kuli on the Turkish side. Chatham inserted a cigarette into the holder and lit it.

Fifteen minutes, twenty minutes, an hour.

By the time someone finally knocked on his door, his eyes burned with the haze of smoke that filled his compartment.

"Your passport, please."

He handed it to the customs official.

"You have contraband?"

"None."

The officer leafed through his passport again. "An archaeologist? You carry no artifacts? Nothing from your excavations?"

"Certainly not."

The customs officer glanced at his luggage in the overhead. "Open your suitcase, please."

Chatham lugged the bag onto the seat and unlocked it.

The officer bent over it, pawed through the contents, and stamped Chatham's passport. "Be careful as you go through Bulgaria. Smugglers and drug dealers transport goods through to Albania and Italy. Watch yourself."

He left Chatham's bag open on the seat and closed the door behind him.

Chatham repacked while the train lurched over the border. It stopped at Svilingrad, where another contingent of officials boarded the train, this time Bulgarians.

When the knock sounded on the door, a uniformed officer leaned into the compartment. "Passport, please."

The officer lounged against the door and thumbed through Chatham's passport, studying page after page. "You must change pounds into leva. One hundred pounds, please." He held out his hand.

"One hundred pounds?" Perhaps the officer had trouble with English, or with the exchange rate. "Are you sure it's a hundred pounds? That's a bit much. I'm only passing through."

"I know the exchange rate. It's in the newspaper every morning." He flashed a sidelong glance at Chatham and closed the passport.

"I read English. After the Russians leave, we all learn English to live." His nose was sharp, his eyes bright blue with a slight bulge. "We have a beautiful country. You may be tempted to stay."

Chatham reached into his pocket for his wallet.

"And sixty pounds for a visa." He peered into Chatham's thick wallet, his hand still out.

Chatham began counting. "You mean leva, don't you?"

"Pounds." The officer watched him detach a hundred-pound note, and waited for sixty more. "And another twenty for the yellow card, *zhelta carta—carte statistique.*"

"I'm only passing through. Staying on the train."

"Nevertheless, those are the rules."

He stamped Chatham's passport and folded a slip of paper inside, then hesitated, still holding the passport. "You forgot the commission."

"Commission?"

"For exchange. That's ten pounds."

Chatham traded his passport for another ten-pound note. "Where are the leva?"

"Leva?"

"I just changed one hundred pounds for leva."

"So you did," the officer said. He reached into his pocket for a roll of bills and handed Chatham three thousand leva.

"What's the exchange rate?" Chatham asked.

"That's the official rate, minus the commission."

"But I already paid the commission."

"So you did," the officer said and turned to go. "We have to inspect all the cars. There's a long delay, two, three hours maybe. You can get off the train, take a walk through the town. Just over the River Maritsa, over the stone bridge."

"But my suitcase."

"I can store it in the baggage car." He tied a ticket to the handle of Chatham's bag and handed him the stub. "Five pounds, please."

Chatham stood up, anxious to walk off some of his irritation. "It's permitted to leave the train?"

"I suggest you do. We have no buffet car on the train." The officer reached for Chatham's suitcase. "There's The English Pub and a hotel in Svilingrad. You can get a good lunch at either."

Chatham started into the corridor.

The customs officer followed. "Be careful of the local *bortsi*."

"*Bortsi*?"

"Mafioso."

Chatham stepped onto the platform and descended the steps to the berm. He walked along the track for some distance before he found a path shaded by overarching linden, the cloying odor of their flowers as overpowering as jasmine. He followed the path to a stone bridge and crossed over it into a town that looked like it came out of a fairy tale from his childhood.

Cherry trees, their red fruit punctuating their leaves like polka dots, lined cobblestone streets. Storks nested in the chimneys of slate roofs. White houses trimmed with dark wood and swathed in grapevines tethered to their broad upper-story overhangs seemed to appear and hide again along the cobbled lanes like women flirting behind fans.

In the town square, old men played cards under the elm trees. Across the square, in front of The English Pub, men in rumpled suits and body-builders in tank shirts, arms crossed and muscles bulging, sat at tables over coffee and worry beads.

Smugglers? Mafia? Chatham hesitated.

He entered the hotel instead. He ate a lunch of vegetable soup flavored with dill and yogurt and bread still warm from the oven. It stuck in his throat as he recalled his last conversation with Emma this morning before he left.

"Love?" she had said. "The only thing you love about me is my father's money."

He had been tempted to tell her that the money was her principal charm. Instead he laid the phone down on the table and went into the bathroom to clean his teeth. When he came back into the room to dress, he became aware of the bleat of a disconnected telephone line. He put the phone back in the cradle just as a knock sounded at the door. It was the bellboy. "Your telephone, sir…."

"I've taken care of it. It was off the hook." He had rummaged on the dresser for a few Turkish lira and handed them to the boy before he closed the door.

After lunch, Chatham wandered through the hotel lobby, looking for a shop with English books. He found stalls with icons, gaudy with gold; antique silver teaspoons; old clocks. The books were all in Bulgarian, printed in the Cyrillic alphabet.

He strolled back to the train along the same path he had taken into town and began to feel blisters form against the heels of his shoes.

He reached the train, anxious to find his compartment, take off his shoes and nurse his feet.

When he opened the compartment door, he discovered a woman curled into the corner of the seat, near the window—a beautiful woman wearing a cheap summer dress and a spiral bracelet the deep burnished yellow of ancient gold on her upper arm. The bracelet had a horse's head and bit decorating one end and a coiled tail on the other.

And on the seat next to her lay the cardboard suitcase with the scratch across it.

Chapter Four

Tepe Hazarfen, Turkey, August 7, 1990

Tamar stared at the rubble in disbelief. Clods of dirt and bits of broken concrete filled the area where the mosaic should have been.

She dropped to her knees and scratched at the ground with her trowel. "Must be under all this." Her voice fluttered with desperation and she continued to scrape.

Mustafa knelt down next to her. He pointed to a cut mark in the concrete in front of them. "Look here," he said and pointed further away. "And here. You see the gouges? Chisel marks. Rolled up overnight and stolen."

"Rolled up? How?"

"They slather the surface of the mosaic with heavy glue, cover it with a canvas, loosen it from the matrix with chisels, and roll it up, bit by bit. I've seen the same thing at other sites. Professional thieves. They work in teams of three or four."

Tamar stood up and walked over the site, eyes on the ground. Chisel marks slashed the surface where the floor should be. "I thought they cut mosaics into transportable sections with a saw."

"Too much noise," Mustafa said. "Rolling it up is more difficult, but quieter, can be done in the night without making a stir."

The theft was as personal to Tamar as an assault. "Why would anyone do this?"

"For the money of course," Mustafa said. "A museum or a New York collector will pay as much as a million, a million and a half dollars for a mosaic floor."

"And no one in the village heard them?"

"That is odd, isn't it?" Orman said and fingered his chin the way he did when he was puzzled or concerned. "Maybe someone in the village...."

His finger brushed back and forth across his chin. "We'll go down to the coffeehouse," he said. "Listen, ask a few questions, see what people are saying."

"I'll stay here," Tamar told them. "Women don't go to village coffeehouses." She sat on the ground, discouraged. "I'll guard the mosaic now that it's gone."

"You could wander around the village, talk to some of the women. See what they say."

"I'll stay here and mope."

She watched Orman and Mustafa start down to the coffeehouse and listened to the dogs bark in Mustafa's wake and wondered if the villagers would talk in front of a stranger like Mustafa.

The loss of the mosaic made her feel abandoned and vaguely chastised, as if she were a child who had done something wrong. She sat, knees up, arms folded, and rocked back and forth.

Sunlight reflected on something on the far side of the ruined floor and caught her eye. She stood up to examine it more closely and crossed the empty ground where the mosaic had been.

It was a white *tessera*. From the mosaic border, she thought. She kept walking, following a faint trail to the back of the tel and away from the village. A large footprint with heavy tread marks pointed toward the steep slope behind the site. She kept going in the direction of the footprint, noting the tamped-down grass. She reached the small escarpment where the site dropped off. She kneeled to examine the edge and detected what looked like rope marks in three places along the rim of the escarpment. They used a pulley, she thought.

Some loose *tesserae* lay on the ground below. She slid down the short, steep slope and continued across the grass, watching for signs of recent disturbance, bending and tilting her head to see the surface of the dry grass from a different angle.

She found the impress of tire tracks and matted-down grass where a vehicle had turned around and a small puddle of grease where it had parked.

She hesitated, then picked up the loose *tesserae*, put them in her pocket and began to clamber back up the escarpment, grabbing for roots, searching for toeholds. Her hat slipped off and dropped to the ground below. She watched it fall, and let it lie there.

When she reached the top, she lay on the grass a moment to catch her breath, her arm shielding her face from the sun. Someone in the village must be involved. The looters must have known where to go, how to get here the back way. And the equipment. They came prepared. You don't wander around the countryside with all that equipment on the off chance that you'll find a mosaic floor in the middle of the night.

For a moment, she thought she heard something stir in the grass, sat up to see what it was, and watched a channel in the dry grass undulate as some creature moved through it. Behind her, she heard Orman and Mustafa climbing up from the village.

"What are you doing lying in the sun?" Orman called to her from across the site.

"Cultivating skin cancer." She rose to greet them. "What did they say? Did they know anything about it in the village?"

"They complained about noises in the night and dogs barking all night long. Mostly, the barking annoyed them. The general consensus was that a man and a woman met for a night of dalliance. No one wants to talk about it because it could end in violence, even murder."

"So much for Sherlock Holmes and dogs that bark in the night."

"The looters must have been strangers," Mustafa said.

She nodded. "But how did they know about the mosaic? Know how to get here?" She turned toward the back of the site. "Come on, I want to show you something." She signaled for them to follow and indicated the footprint.

Mustafa put his shoe beside it. "Must be a big fellow, two meters or more. His shoes are a good four centimeters longer than mine."

"There are other footprints," she said, and pointed to another trail of footsteps beside them, smaller in size.

"Another member of the team," Mustafa said.

She led them to the rope marks from pulleys along the cliff face, and pointed to the tire tracks and oil stain below. "Right there, beyond my hat. A large vehicle, with wide tires, probably some kind of truck. They came prepared."

"How do you know the marks are from last night?" Mustafa asked.

She pulled the *tesserae* from her pocket. "I found these on the ground next to the tire tracks."

Mustafa looked at the *tesserae* in her hand and lifted his arms as if making an offering. "You have to understand what something like this means to a poor peasant. Whatever he got for the floor was probably more than he could earn in three years. It could mean survival, the difference between starvation and just getting by."

"And if an archaeologist gets in the way of the transaction," Tamar said, "what then?" Her voice caught when she remembered that horrible night in the Yucatan. "What then?" she asked again. "Kill the archaeologist?"

"That doesn't happen," Mustafa said. "The poor peasant needs to eat. It's better to feed starving people than hide tomb offerings in a rich museum where they gather dust in a dark cupboard for years."

For a moment, she forgot Hazarfen and the villa and remembered only that long night in Meride in the Yucatan. She remembered every moment of it, remembered her toes pinching in her high-heeled shoes as she paced the hallway, remembered the smooth feel of the silk shawl against her bare shoulders. She and Alex were going to celebrate, a double celebration for their first anniversary and for Alex's discovery of the lost site of Katamul hidden in the jungle. They were going to dine in the roof garden on lobster and champagne, make love all night, and wake up in the morning smiling.

She was still holding out the *tesserae*. "I know how it operates in the Yucatan. A poor peasant finds a 'specimen,' a 'tomb furnishing' when he plows his field, and he knows it's worth more than his cash crops. He sells it to an *estelero*. The *estelero* sells it to a dealer in Meride for twice the price, who sells it to a dealer in Mexico City where it doubles again. That dealer smuggles it into Los Angeles. Now the price really escalates, three, four times. The L.A. dealer sells it to a movie star for ten times the price. The movie star donates it to the museum, which evaluates it at double what she paid for it. Everybody's happy. Everybody makes a tidy profit, and the movie star gets a hefty tax write-off."

Mustafa reached for the *tesserae* and stashed them in his hip pocket. His clenched fist in his pocket made an outline against his hip. "What we dig up goes from one hole in the ground to another, ends up in the basement of a museum. In the end, no one remembers anything about the artifact and the archaeologist's notes are torn and scattered and eaten by worms." He took his hand out of his pocket and said in his significant voice, "These things should be seen, give others an appreciation of the past."

"You're as cynical as Chatham."

Mustafa squatted near the rope marks, running his hands along the dry grass along the edge of the cliff. "I'm not saying I approve of it. I'm just saying that I can understand how it happens."

Tamar had started back toward the missing mosaic when she heard the stirring in the grass again. It sounded like the parched scraping of a rope along the dry ground. The grass shifted again, this time closer, moving toward Mustafa with a hissing sound.

She saw a black snake loom out of the grass behind Mustafa, coiled and ready to strike.

Instinctively, she grabbed a cobble from the ruined floor. "Don't move," she shouted, and hurled the projectile at the head of the snake. The rock flew past Orman, past the startled Mustafa and hit the snake squarely in its gaping mouth.

The crushed head of the snake collapsed onto the grass.

Mustafa was still at the edge of the cliff, white-faced, staring at the bloody remnants of the shattered snake with a mixture of horror and regret.

"You killed it," he said.

"Of course she did," Orman said.

"You shouldn't have done that. It was a snake. A black snake."

"What's wrong with you?" Orman said. "It was about to attack you."

"Still. She killed it."

"And saved your life," Orman said. He turned to Tamar. "I didn't see the rock coming. How'd you do that? You could have hit one of us."

"I'm a pretty good pitcher," she said, but she was still shaking. "I taught myself."

"Taught yourself to kill the occasional snake? You threw that rock at from at least four meters away at the head of the snake and hit it."

"I had brothers. Whenever they went somewhere, they never took me. 'You're too young,' they would tell me. 'You're only a girl.'"

"So you taught yourself to throw things?"

"I decided to show them. They liked baseball, so I hung a tire from the branch of a lemon tree and practiced throwing the ball through the tire from ten feet away, then twenty feet, finally the full sixty-six. Then I used smaller and smaller targets, ended up throwing the ball through an embroidery hoop." She smiled and rubbed her wrist. "Then I went for speed and power. I got so good, they brought me to all their games and let me pitch. Until—" Her voice trailed off.

"Until what?" Orman asked.

"Never mind," she said. "It doesn't matter." But she noticed that her hand was shaking. She made a fist and shoved her hand in her pocket so that no one would notice. "Anyway," she said. "We always slaughtered the other team."

"Like you slaughtered the snake," Mustafa said. "You shouldn't have killed it."

"Why not?" Orman asked.

Mustafa sighed and inhaled slowly. "In the old religions, you know, snakes were sacred. Snakes are special creatures. They shed their skins and renew themselves again and again."

Orman played with his mustache. "You're Yezidi."

"What's Yezidi?" Tamar asked.

"Devil worshippers," Orman said.

Mustafa's nostrils flared. "Not devil worshippers."

Tamar was puzzled by his anger. She held out her hand in a helpless gesture, trying to calm him.

He backed away. "Don't touch me."

"Nobody thinks you worship the devil," she told him.

"The snake wasn't poisonous," he said. His face was red and his voice heavy with agitation. "It would never hurt anyone."

Tamar watched him. She was tempted to reach out again, then thought better of it.

"About the mosaic," she said after a while. "We don't have pictures. I usually take record shots with a Polaroid, but I didn't have time."

"You and Orman are the only ones who know what the mosaic looks like?"

"It was the last day and we ran out of film, I thought your people could—"

"Without pictures, how do you expect to find it?" Mustafa asked.

"Tamar and I can go after it, identify it," Orman said. "That's the only way."

"You think they took it to Istanbul?" Tamar asked.

Orman looked at her, shaking his head. "It's long gone from Turkey by now. Probably shipped out through the Balkans, ending up in one of the big antiquities markets, Basel or Berlin."

"You'll never find it," Mustafa said.

"Things are missing from Ephesus too," Orman said. "Maybe Kosay at the museum there has some ideas." He ran a finger along his chin and rubbed his upper lip. "We'll stop there first. Then

I'll go to Berlin," he said. "Tamar to Basel, see what's hitting the antiquities market, see if we come up with the mosaic."

Tamar shook her head. "I couldn't do that. I don't know anything about the antiquities market. I wouldn't know where to start."

Orman rubbed his chin again. "What was it American archaeologists used to say in the '60s? Archaeology is anthropology or it is nothing.' You were trained as an anthropologist. Do a little anthropological fieldwork, a little participant observation. Nothing bad will happen to you." He leaned toward her. "It's Switzerland, where they yodel. The land of Heidi and chocolate bars."

"Besides, nobody kills anthropologists," Mustafa said. "Or archaeologists, for that matter."

"Except Binali," Orman said.

Tamar took a deep breath. "And others."

That night in Meride seared her memory. Out of the corner of her eye, she saw Orman signal to Mustafa and glance toward her.

"Oh," Mustafa said. "You said the Yucatan. *That* Saticoy. Alexander Saticoy?"

Tamar remembered her last sight of him, standing in front of a stele in Katamul, notebook in hand, giving her a quick wink, a wave goodbye, and a smile as she walked toward the truck. "Yes. Alex. You heard about it here in Turkey?"

"I was at the Society of American Archaeology meeting in San Francisco that year. It was the talk of the meetings."

"You were at the SAA?" Orman asked.

"I'm a museum man, not a field archaeologist. There was a special session on setting up a worldwide computerized registration code and network. I was at the British Museum that year, and it was my turn to go."

While Mustafa spoke, Orman watched Tamar, his eyes narrowed and speculative.

"You owe it to other archaeologists to do whatever you can to stop the looting," Orman said to her. "To Binali and to Alex."

"To make the world safe for archaeology?"

"And archaeologists," Orman said gently.

And for those who wait anxiously through the endless darkness of long nights in Meride with the cloying scent of night-blooming jasmine, with the humid air heavy as doom.

"I'll go," she said at last.

Chapter Five

Svilingrad, Bulgaria, August 7, 1990

Chatham hesitated at the compartment door to check the number. It was his compartment, all right.

"Who are you?" he asked the woman in his seat. "What are you doing here?"

The woman looked up at him with a shy smile, then shrugged. "We say in Bulgaria, 'Every train has its travelers.'"

Her voice was velvety and musical—like the rest of her, he thought, with her creamy olive skin, the soft curve of her cheek, her slate blue eyes. My God, she was beautiful.

The train began to move, throwing him off balance. He gripped the doorframe, tried to steady himself. The train lurched away from the platform and he staggered into the compartment toward the seat opposite her. When it jolted to a stop, he fell forward on one knee, feeling awkward and foolish.

"I don't mind riding backwards," he said and felt even more foolish.

She lowered her eyes and her dark lashes brushed against her cheek. Chatham thought he detected a tear. A strand of hair, soft and glossy, cascaded across her face and danced with the movement of the train. He reached out to touch it and pulled back just in time.

He wondered again who she was, how she got into his compartment. He wondered about the bracelet on her arm with the horse's head. Thracian, maybe.

She lifted her head and moved her hand with liquid grace to tuck the strand behind her ear. Her fingers were long and slender, her arms silky smooth.

She gave him another smile and crossed her legs. The train jerked forward again. The compartment door slammed shut with the sudden movement and the train heaved out of the station.

He waited for the woman to speak while they swayed with the motion of the train.

"You must help me, Professor Chatham," she said at last.

"You know who I am?"

"I waited for you. I need your help."

"Who are you?"

"I am called Irena." She hesitated. She was shaking. "You must help. You are our only hope." Her lip quivered and she extended her hand in a beseeching gesture.

How delicate she was, how vulnerable. "I don't understand."

"I must show you."

She clicked open the latch on the suitcase and lifted the lid. The case was packed with parcels wrapped in newspaper. She waited a moment. For drama, he thought. He watched the nervous slide of her tongue across her upper lip before she reached for a parcel, unwrapped it and held up a pair of elaborate gold earrings with a galloping horse and a small worked amphora dangling from the loop. She laid them on the seat beside her. Then she opened another—a golden laurel wreath—and still another—a necklace with a bull pendant.

He leaned forward and caught his breath. It was Thracian gold, all right, all of it.

The Thracians had villages and cities along the Euxine Sea: the Black Sea today. Even the fabled Byzantium, long before it became the gilded city where Constantine built his marvels and monuments to rule his empire, had been a Thracian settlement.

"Thracian, like the bracelet wrapped around your arm?" he asked. Thracians, the wild people of the north, Herodotus had said. They came from the land where the Boreal winds blew, and they had gold.

She moved her head in assent. "The bracelet is very rare." She lifted her right hand to stroke the horse's head on her arm and he envied her fingers.

When he reached over to examine one of the earrings, he brushed against her knee. He held the gold between his fingers and traced the magnificent workmanship.

"Beautiful, beautiful," he said. "Where did you get these pieces?"

"Are they worth a great deal?"

"A museum or a collector would pay a lot of money for this at auction, but—" He hesitated. "I'm an archaeologist, I can't help you sell it."

He put down the earring and picked up the delicate laurel wreath and looked over at her. Thracian women, according to Herodotus, were promiscuous and dripped with gold. The thought sent a tingle of desire through him. This time, he brushed against her thigh.

"Where did you get these?" he asked again.

She seemed distraught, concentrating on what she had to say, as her lashes brushed her cheeks again. "It's all we have left," she began in a low voice.

He had to lean forward to listen, one hand reaching across the space between them to rest on her thigh. Carefully, she took his hand in hers, uncrossed her legs and crossed them again while he watched.

She told him how her brother found a tomb on the grounds of their country house, and Chatham watched the seductive movement of her lips as she carefully pronounced each word.

She told him how she and her brother had gone out each night to dig in the tomb, bringing back the treasure piece by piece to hide in her room, and Chatham wondered how it would feel to stroke her silken skin.

She talked about the mansion where she was raised, about the dark wood paneling, about the broad staircase, the seat below the stained glass window at the landing where she would sit and read, and Chatham savored the motion of her crossed legs and watched her thighs, tight against her flimsy dress, swaying with the movement of the train.

Thracian gold, he thought, and only I know about it. I can publish the find, make a name for myself, became a star of Near Eastern archaeology. With that, and my other project, I can be free of Emma, out of bondage at last.

"When the Communists took over," she was saying, "they took everything." And he watched her uncross her legs and let her gently pry the laurel wreath from his hand before she wrapped the newspaper around it again.

She told him how her father had died, drunk with grief, stumbling on the ice in front of a speeding car. She described her mother's last days, hungry and gasping for breath, during that same cold relentless winter.

"Irena," he said, enchanted with the sound of her name. "Irena," he repeated and longed to console her, to brush the tears from her cheeks, to enfold her in comforting arms.

She kept talking and he was overwhelmed by the thrum of her anguished voice, the music of it slithering through his soul, the rocking of the train mesmerizing him until he was lost in a cloud of desire.

The screech of brakes jolted him out of his haze, and for a moment he thought of Lilith, the Screech Owl Goddess with the feathered legs, and remembered Emma.

"Where are we?" he asked.

"Plovdiv," she said.

The train stumbled to a stop. Passengers waiting at the edge of the platform seemed to waver in the currents of air that eddied around the slowing train and backed away as the conductor lowered the steps. A milling crowd, waving leva and shouting for attention, surrounded an old woman selling sandwiches and bottled drinks in the far corner of the platform.

"I haven't eaten for two days," Irena told him.

"There's a sandwich vendor out there," Chatham said. He knew that she had seen the old woman, but he said it anyway. "I'll get you something." That was the least he could do for her. "Be right back."

Chatham lingered at the edge of the crowd, trying to find the end of the queue. Hands and arms reached over him, passing money and plastic-wrapped sandwiches back and forth over his head. No queue, just a wild grab of confusion. He pushed his way forward, almost overwhelmed by the smell of body heat, snatched a sandwich from the basket and threw down a ten leva note.

He made his way back to the train just as the conductor pulled up the steps, and hurried toward the compartment.

Irena was gone. The suitcase and Irena, both gone. Only a card was left on the seat.

He looked out the compartment door and searched the passageway. The train began to move. He stumbled to the window and searched the platform. No sign of her. The platform receded as the train picked up speed. He hoped for a glimpse of her, waving, calling, running after the train. He would pull the emergency cord and rescue her, reach for her, pull her onto the train, her body close against his, warm and damp from the effort of running. The train emerged into the open air, into the countryside, and still he stood at the window, searching, hoping.

Finally, he picked up the card and sat in her seat to catch the warmth of her, the scent of her.

The card was printed in Cyrillic on one side and English on the other. It said:

Irena Konstantinova
Ulitza G.S. Rakovsky 10
Blok 4, Entrance g, Floor 3, Apt. 26
Sofia

He held the card between his fingers and pictured holding her lovely face between his hands, imagined stroking the sleek softness of her skin. He stared into the space in front of him and summoned up the seductive sound of her voice, the graceful movement of her hands.

Her presence haunted him. He gazed out the window at the hills and plane trees and saw the flutter of her hair in the stir of the leaves, the motion of her lashes in the gentle movement of tufts of grass in the breeze. He closed his eyes to remember more, hoping, as he lingered on the edge of sleep, to dream of her.

He woke to the caw, caw, caw of a screech owl. Emma, angry again. He opened his eyes, feeling as if he had slept all night. His mouth was dry and he was disoriented, surprised that it was still daylight. He was on a train, he remembered. The noise was the bleat of the train signaling that they were going around a curve.

It was strange, he thought, Emma as Lilith, the screech owl.

He remembered a session on ancient mythology at a meeting on Near Eastern archaeology. One of the papers recounted an ancient Hebrew myth about Lilith as God's mistake, created before Adam and Eve. The man delivering the paper said that Lilith gave birth only to monsters because she was asexual, that God banished her to Eilat and created Adam and Eve, man and woman, in her stead. The man giving the paper smirked and said the story wasn't in the Scriptures because the redactors believed God shouldn't make mistakes.

Chatham thought of Emma as the child of Lilith and almost laughed out loud. He was fully awake now.

He still held Irena's card in his hand. He wondered whether she was in danger, whether the card was a cry for help.

He pushed the button to call the porter and told him that he wanted his suitcase from the baggage car and gave him the chit.

He waited for the porter to come back and pictured Irena again and again and felt inexplicably giddy with joy.

The porter returned with the suitcase and dumped it on the seat across from Chatham.

"Ten leva, please," he said and Chatham gave him twelve.

He thought of Emma, lying in the sun in a beach chair at Bodrum, her blonde hair stiff with bleach, her leathery tanned skin, her bony shoulders, and he got off the train at Sofia.

He'd find Irena, he vowed, and he'd find the gold.

He plunged into the chaos and milling crowds of the station and stopped at a stall to buy flowers.

"Half a dozen roses, please," he said in English, wondering if the flower seller could understand him.

A dog, its coat dusty and unkempt, sniffed at his trousers and then scratched its fleas as it scraped its back along the sidewalk.

"So many..." the woman hesitated, seemed to be searching for words, "strange dogs on the street in Sofia," the woman said. "People can't afford to feed pets, so they go loose and run in packs. Not too scary in the day, but at night they attack."

He paid the woman two leva and found a cab in the taxi rank. The driver had stepped out of the cab and said to him in English, "I take you wherever you wish."

Another enterprising Bulgarian, Chatham thought, who replaced Russian with English for the tourist trade.

The cab driver tried to smile. He had steely blue eyes and a scar that reached across his cheek to his upper lip. It made him look like he was sneering, and Chatham felt sorry for him.

"Ulitza G.S. Rakovski," he said and showed the driver the card with Irena's address.

"I know where it is," the driver said. "Near the city garden."

"I need a receipt," Chatham said.

The driver looked back at him, tore a slip of paper from a pad, and handed it back to him.

"The meter," Chatham told him. "Set the meter."

"It's broken."

"How much to Ulitza Rakovsky?"

"Fifty leva."

"Fifty?" He had to go to her, to save her from God knows what, he thought to himself. He shrugged and said okay.

They drove down broad avenues created for parades, past blocks of large, dreary concrete apartment buildings, their facades cracked and peeling.

"The Palace of Culture," the driver said, gesturing to a building on the right. "When the Russians were here, there was a large ruby and gold star on the top that shone in the night. After they left, someone stole it. People get rich now from stealing."

"I'll give you sixty leva if you get me there faster."

"Okay. I hurry." The driver waved his hand to the left. "Here we have many museums. I show you Sofia."

Why had she left so suddenly, with no word?

"Ulitza G.S. Rakovsky," Chatham said.

They passed a many-domed building, as pretentious as a dowager, its copper and gilded cupolas glinting in the sun.

Maybe she didn't want to see him. But she left the card.

"The Cathedral of Saint Alexander Nevsky," the taxi driver said, waving at the building.

The taxi began to circumvent the cathedral while Chatham wondered what Irena was afraid of, why she left so suddenly.

"The cathedral has a museum for icons in the basement," the driver said. "You like icons? Bulgaria is famous for icons. I can get you an old one by a famous artist, cheap. You want?"

"I want Rakovsky Street."

They had gone all around the cathedral by now and were starting a second circuit.

"I can get you anything else you need in Sofia." The driver slowed the taxi, reached into his pocket, and turned to face Chatham. "Anything," he repeated. "You want my card? I give you my card."

Chatham waved it away. "Rakovsky Street. Now."

The driver shrugged, turned back to the wheel and started around the park behind the cathedral. He stopped in front of a large, square block of dilapidated stucco buildings.

"Ulitza G.S. Rakofsky ten," he said, "as you wished."

Chatham threw fifty leva into the front seat, grabbed his suitcase and bolted from the taxi. He searched for building numbers and finally found blue metal markers attached to the corner of each building just above the ground floor windows. He looked for Building 4, Entrance G. That must be gamma in Cyrillic, he thought, gamma. He ran inside and reached for the banister. It pulled from the wall into his hand.

He sprinted up the stairs to the first landing, reached for the button to light the stairwell. It didn't work. He dashed up another flight. This time when he pushed the button, a weak light flickered in the hallway. He ran up to the third floor landing and looked for apartment 26 in the dim light. He made his way down the hall, past doorway after doorway, 20, 22, and finally 26. He could just make out a strip of cardboard in the wavering light with the name Konstantinov in Cyrillic and Latin script taped on the door. He pushed the bell.

The man from the railway station in Istanbul opened the door.

Chapter Six

Ephesus, Turkey, August 8, 1990

"Terrible thing about Binali," Kosay was saying.

They were standing in the peristyle of an ancient Roman villa, surrounded by columns and a portico. The courtyard, open to the sky in the center of the house, gave light to all the rooms. They stood next to a shallow rectangular basin, an *impluvium*, built to catch water that ran off the roof to provide water for household tasks.

Tamar, Orman, and Mustafa had clambered up the stairs with Kosay along the narrow lanes that separated the villas, above the remains of shops and taverns on the lowest level, to the slope above the Street of the Curetes so that Kosay could check the work on the restoration of one of the villas in the part of the city where prosperous Ephesians lived.

"It's for tourism, you know," Kosay told them. "To make it authentic as possible to show life in Ephesus in the Late Roman period during the heyday of Ephesus when Artemis still ruled. Before she was replaced by Christianity."

On the way up, they had paused once to take a picture of a manhole that gave access to sewer pipes that led from the houses and was stamped with SPQR, the logo of the Roman Empire.

Earlier that day, they had visited the house of the Virgin Mary on a wooded knoll on Bülbül Daği, the Mountain of the Nightingales, above the Magnesia Gate.

Kosay had swept his arm in the direction of Ephesus and said, "You can just make it out from here, the road from the old harbor. Today, the harbor is three miles away," Kosay said. "Once, the road from the harbor was lined with shops and grand public buildings." He shook his head. "No more."

For a moment Tamar visualized him standing on the hilltop in the twilight after the tourists had left, presiding over Ephesus while the ghosts of the past whispered and whipped like wind through the grand boulevards and broken temples of the Ephesians. She almost expected him to say, "Mine, all mine, as far as the eye can see."

Instead, he said, "During the vernal equinox, pilgrims would crowd into Ephesus from all parts of the empire for the week-long festival in honor of the goddess, pouring through the city gates and along the broad avenues. They shopped in the market stalls, bargaining for jewelry and small statues of the goddess, some of silver, some of gold and ivory with onyx hands and faces. They patronized the brothels, the baths. They used the public toilets.

"In those days Ephesus was crammed with pilgrims from all over the Roman world. They came in the spring for the Vernal Festival to honor the beautiful Artemis, the Virgin Mother of the Gods, to walk along the Street of the Curetes, to marvel at the fountains and the grandeur of the temples, most of all the Temple of Artemis."

He paused. "It was burnt by the Goths," he said.

"The Ephesians were clever, you know. After Constantine, when the pilgrims stopped coming, all was not lost for the enterprising Ephesians. St. John, author of the Revelations, spent the last years of his life in Ephesus and is buried on the hill up there."

He pointed toward a hill in Selçuk that overlooked Ephesus. "His tomb became a place of pilgrimage.

"Soon they began to circulate rumors that Mary had come to visit John and spent her last years here. And that's not all," he went on. "In the nineteenth century an Austrian nun had a dream in which she saw the house of the Virgin Mary, located up there. When the Austrian archaeologists came to dig, they found the house exactly where the nun said it would be, exactly how she described it."

He looked over at them with a smile. "It was built in the sixth century. Mary must have lived a miraculously long and sanctified life." He lifted a quizzical eyebrow. "In the twentieth century, the popes declared the house a place of pilgrimage."

He gestured toward the trees surrounding the house, strung with prayers left by visitors to the holy site.

"They say that Mary not only spent her last days here, she is also buried here."

"She's buried in Jerusalem, in the Kidron Valley, across from St. Stephan's Gate," Tamar said.

"Mary is buried in many places. She died well, and she died often, and according to the Italians, she never died at all, but went straight to heaven with her shoes on."

He paused a moment for an expressive shrug. "Christians outside of Ephesus knew nothing about this before the Council of Ephesus. Early travelers such as the Bordeaux Pilgrim and Egeria, a pilgrim from Aquitaine, visited Ephesus but never alluded to Mary in connection with the city."

They drove down the hill, stopping once at a souvenir kiosk, where Tamar bought a guidebook, a set of slides for lectures, and a statuette of Diana of Ephesus to put on the dashboard of her car, and then continued on to the main part of the site where Kosay was supervising the reconstruction of one of the Roman villas on the slope.

Kosay inspected the remains of a fountain on the north side of the peristyle in the Roman house on the slope before he spoke again.

"Binali called me from Kilis, you know," he said. "He was upset, said something was very wrong, that he had to see me."

"Did he tell you what upset him?" Mustafa asked.

"He didn't want to say over the phone. I told him to come ahead."

"And then?" Orman asked.

Kosay shrugged and sighed. "He was killed before I could see him."

"And the Kybele," Orman said. "It was stolen the same day?"

"Appalling. There's a rash of thefts. The Kybele, the mosaic from your site."

"If you're not careful," Orman said, "they'll steal your streets."

"It's not a joke, Orman. I take my job as a custodian of the past seriously."

"As we all do," Orman said.

Kosay led them through the Roman house from room to room, all lit by an eerie light that filtered through splintered roofs. He pointed out frescoes of muses and patterned mosaic floors, water closets and fountains, as if he were a real estate agent showing an extravagant house in a California suburb.

"They lived in luxury with kitchens and baths, central heating and running water," he told them.

"The best of everything," Mustafa said, with a touch of envy and maybe a tinge of disapproval for their dissolute ways.

Tamar had heard somewhere that Mustafa came from the mountains of Kurdistan, where even running water was a luxury.

When Kosay finished, he led them down to the Street of the Curetes, named for the priests of the terrible Anatolian goddess Kybele.

"This is where Binali was killed," he said, pausing for a moment, pointing to a spot on the ground where the soil between the tesserae had darkened, and then went on down the street.

In front of the arched entrance to Hadrian's Temple, a young Brit had climbed on a plinth to strike a heroic pose, his backpack on the sidewalk, while his friend fidgeted with a camera. A woman with a minicam on her shoulder shouted to them, "Out of the way, out of the way." She turned to Tamar and said, "*Schrecklich*. They are everywhere," before Tamar moved on to join the others as they took a dogleg onto the Marble Road.

Kosay stopped at the corner of the Street of the Curetes and Marble Street next to a footstep incised in the pavement.

"This is the brothel, once filled with laughter. Now only silence," he said. "Under the sand in there, there's a mosaic floor with portraits of the women of the brothel."

He crossed into the brothel and took a whiskbroom from his back pocket. He brushed away the sand that covered the floor to reveal a mosaic portrait of a young woman with a long, melancholy face and dark-rimmed eyes, then he sighed and covered her again and led them further up the street.

They passed the many-columned *agora* and continued on, stopping in front of the theatre.

"This is where bulls and manhood were sacrificed for the glory of Artemis," Kosay said. "And where the Ephesians attacked St. Paul. He stood there, ranting at them, and for three hours they attacked and harassed him, shouting, 'Great is the Artemis of the Ephesians. Great is the Artemis of the Ephesians.' They stoned him, almost killed him, your St. Paul."

He nodded toward Tamar, as if she had sole proprietorship of St. Paul. The accusation made her feel responsible for the decline of Ephesus, made her feel that if it weren't for her, Artemis would still be alive and well, receiving the bloody testicles of bulls and supervising the castration of priests.

They walked a little way along Arcadia Street, the broad colonnaded road paved with marble that once led to the harbor, to the parking lot and got into the van, and started up the road toward Selçuk.

He drove a little way, stopped, and pointed to the ruins of a Byzantine church. "The Church of the Virgin Mary," he said. "It was once a basilica near the port, a commercial exchange in the heyday of Ephesus. They converted it into this church in her honor. They hosted the third Ecumenical Council here at this church and had Mary declared a virgin, the Virgin Mother of God, just as Artemis was the Virgin Mother of the Gods."

"Ephesus," Orman said, "the city of virgins."

They rode past the remains of the stadium, the Byzantine walls, Kosay shaking his head all the while.

At the Selçuk road, he turned, drove up toward the Basilica of St. John, and stopped again.

"The Temple of Artemis," Kosay said, gesturing to a forlorn column standing in a shallow pool of water on their left. "One of the Seven Wonders of the Ancient World, the largest building in the Greek world."

Ducks in the pool sailed past the column and ruffled the surface of the water.

"It was long and narrow, made of marble, surmounted by a pitched roof and pediment with three openings where Artemis would appear suddenly during the festival, awe inspiring and bloody, and lit by the evening sun."

The Mosque of Isa Bey and the ruins of the Basilica of St. John the Apostle loomed on the hill beyond the temple. Overhead, a stork soared, lit on top of the column of the Temple of Artemis, and fluttered her wings.

"Ephesus had always been protected from harm by the gods," Kosay said. "But after Constantine, after the black-robed priests came, nothing was the same. The city never recovered."

"The temple was destroyed by Goths," Orman said.

Kosay pointed a reproachful finger at him. "But never rebuilt. The harbor silted up, earthquakes and fires destroyed much of the grandeur of the city. The Artemesion was deserted. The library of Celsus burnt and stood on the main street of the city as an abandoned shell. The houses on the hill turned into a slum. The magnificent villas were divided and subdivided into tiny hovels with little light and air, the frescoes painted over or broken by partition walls."

Once again, he looked accusingly at Tamar and she shriveled.

"And now we have only ruins," he said.

They had reached the museum by now. He rushed them through the first room filled with findings from the houses: table legs and toys, statuettes and busts, fresco fragments and gods.

Tamar paused, agape at a statue of a male with grotesquely enlarged genitals.

"Priapos," Orman told her. "He was the god of fertility. He stood out in the vineyards like a scarecrow to protect the vines."

"He looks like a disease," Tamar said.

"But he sure scared the crows."

Kosay said, "According to Plutarch, the Ephesians worshipped fecundity," and hustled them through the next hall, filled with gods and carvings from the many fountains of Ephesus. Mustafa lingered behind.

They entered a hall displaying small finds: coins and jewelry, portrait heads and panels.

"The Kybele was stolen from a case in this room," Kosay said.

"Not from the excavation?" Orman asked.

"It was on loan."

"From which site?"

"From a private collector. Anonymous."

"It was insured?"

"That's not the point," Kosay said. "I am responsible for protecting the past, and I failed."

"It was in a locked case?" Mustafa asked.

Kosay shook his head, and made a negative tick with his tongue. "From a case like the one over there."

He gestured toward a case with Plexiglas sides and a waist-high stand that held a single object lit from above.

"It's open on top," Mustafa said.

"You would have to be three meters tall to reach inside," Kosay answered.

"You have a guard?" Mustafa asked.

Kosay indicated an empty chair near the door. "He's from Kusadasi. Sometimes he's late. But he's honest."

"Of course he is," Mustafa said. He walked around the case, eyed the perimeter of the room, tested the resilience of the floor. "No sensors?" he asked.

Kosay shook his head.

"It would take less than a minute to step onto the chair to reach an object in the case," Mustafa said. "You have improved your security since? Put on an extra guard? You will install sensors?"

Kosay looked sheepish. "Not enough money."

"Then what do you expect?" Mustafa asked.

Kosay gave him an injured look and led them out of the room.

They stopped for a moment in the garden and looked at sarcophagi and parapets, sundials and column fragments, and continued through a hall with findings from graves, with Mycenaean pottery and tomb stele, then into the hall of Artemis.

Here he paused in front of a statue of the Great Artemis with a turreted crown, superhuman in form, adorned with fruits and animals and other symbols of fertility, arms outstretched for giving and receiving.

The two statues of Artemis stood at opposite ends of the hall. The Great Artemis wore a crown with three tiers of city walls topped with the representation of a temple. Her legs were encased in a tight skirt decorated with lions, bulls, goats. Her outstretched arms were missing. And an array of bull's testicles adorned her many-breasted chest.

"Our Artemis is no ordinary Artemis, eternally hovering between girlhood and womanhood," Kosay said. "Nor is she entirely the enthroned Kybele, mother of the gods and goddesses, of mountains, caverns, and beasts. She is like no other goddess. She is Mother Nature herself, the Great Virgin Mother of the Gods."

He pointed to her crown and the animals on her skirt. "Those are her attributes," he said. "The lions and the crown on her head, the *polis*."

The Beautiful Artemis stood opposite, arms extended, her hairdo and her skirt decorated with animals, her chest covered with egg-like bull testes. Her *polis* was missing.

They followed Kosay through the courtyard into another gallery and into a small, neat office at the far end. Blooming African daisies lined the window ledge. Kosay reached into a file cabinet and extracted a photograph that he placed on the desk.

Tamar expected the Kybele to resemble the Ephesian Kybele, perhaps, in her guise as Artemis with her turreted crown; perhaps the Neolithic Kybele from Çatal Hüyük, looking like

Queen Victoria enthroned on a birthing stool, a morbidly obese woman with dimpled knees and ham-like arms, 8,000 years old, and counting. But this one was different—a gold statuette of Kybele flanked by two lions, her skirt tight, her hands straight at her side.

Kosay pointed to the *polis* headdress and the lions at her side. "These are also her attributes, the same as those of Artemis, the same as the Mother Goddess from Neolithic Çatal Hüyük. She, too, has lions on either side and the remnants of a *polis* on her head.

"She is credited with giving birth to the land of Anatolia," Kosay was saying. He ran his finger lovingly along the photograph of Kybele, pausing at the lions at her feet. "The religion of the Mother Goddess is the oldest religion in the world."

The words and music of a song began roiling through Tamar's head while he spoke.

Give me that old-time religion,
Give me that old-time religion.
It's good enough for me.

"Not all ancient religions believed in a Mother Goddess," Mustafa said. "Fertility comes from the male." He rumbled on. "Some people are the descendants of Adam alone. They know that life comes from Adam, the father of us all."

Orman gave him a disapproving look sharp enough to wither the virility of a bull.

In the silence that followed, Tamar thought of Artemis with her bloody apron, of Mary in her house on the hill, of the grossly exaggerated genitals of Priapos in the museum halls, and the song kept buzzing through her head.

It was good enough for mother,
It was good enough for father,
And it's good enough for me.

Chapter Seven

Sofia, Bulgaria, August 7, 1990

Chatham felt a twinge of apprehension at the sight of the man from the train. His bulk filled the doorway. His stance held an unspoken threat.

How did he get to Sofia so quickly? Did he stay on the train?

"Professor Chatham?" the man said in a low, rumbling voice. He had bulging eyes and a jutting chin.

"You're Konstantinov?" The man nodded. "Irena's brother?"

He looked at the roses. "You come to see my sister?" He opened the door wider and stood back.

Chatham stood awkwardly in the hall, his suitcase in his hand, the flowers held in front of him like a buffer. He blustered with courage he didn't feel and tightened his grip on the bouquet of roses.

"Where is Irena? She disappeared from the train."

The man stood aside. Behind him was a long whitewashed passageway trimmed with dark wood. A door opened at the far end. Irena drifted through and sailed toward Chatham, her arms spread out to greet him.

For a moment, Chatham felt a tic of anxiety. Then, watching her glide down the hall with her sweet smile of welcome, he was reassured.

He held out the bouquet.

"Come in, come in," Irena said. "My brother Dimitar and I expected you."

With a deft motion she maneuvered him into the apartment and closed the door behind him.

He put down his bag and once more offered the flowers. "You knew I was coming?"

"I saw a spider spin his web in the window. In Bulgaria, that's always a sign of a visitor. And when I set the table, I laid out an extra place by mistake. That too is a sign."

"You got off the train. How did you get here before me?"

"My brother met me with a car in Plovdiv. I didn't tell you?" Her hand was on his arm now. "I'm glad you came. I wanted to see you again."

She reached for the flowers, brushed them lightly against her cheek, and buried her perfect nose next to a rose. He wanted to say, "You are so beautiful, even roses blush when they see you." The words would have sounded insincere and sophomoric, so he said nothing. Instead, his face flushed with embarrassment.

"An even number of flowers is for a funeral," she said and pulled one rose out of the bouquet. She snapped the stem to shorten it, and moving closer, inserted the rose into the buttonhole of his lapel. "There now," she said and patted his chest. "Of course you will stay for dinner?"

Irena led him to a fairly large room at the end of the corridor furnished with a dingy rug, a table with four ladder-back chairs and a lumpy sofa that looked like it doubled as a bed.

The table was set for three, Chatham noticed. She really did expect him.

Irena told her brother she must go to the *pazara*, the market, to buy food for dinner, and Dimitar reached into his pocket and took out a few leva. Chatham recalled Irena's conversation on the train, her resigned admission of their poverty. Her hospitality might cost them a meal later.

"Allow me," he said and held out twenty leva with a flourish, feeling gallant and generous.

"Oh, no, not necessary," Dimitar said as Irena reached for the twenty leva note and stashed it in her purse. She told Chatham to sit, to make himself at home, to speak with Dimitar, to get acquainted. Then she left.

Chatham and Dimitar sat near the table in the ladder-back chairs, not quite facing each other. They looked at the table, at their fingers, out the window at the cloudless sky. Chatham felt the sharp edge from the corner of the chair press into his thigh, and moved his leg. He glanced at Dimitar, seeking some resemblance to Irena in Dimitar's once-handsome face. A network of tiny broken veins gave his cheeks a pink tinge. Broken by time and slivovitz, Chatham thought.

Dimitar reached into his pocket, took out a package of Rothmans, and offered one to Chatham. Chatham shook his head and waved the cigarette away with thanks. Dimitar stood up, brought an ashtray to the table, and sat down again.

"Cigarettes are expensive in Bulgaria?" Chatham asked.

"Everything is expensive." He flourished the cigarette in the air between two fingers. "Other countries have a brain drain. In Bulgaria we have a money drain. A bank drain. All the money in Bulgaria is in the treasury of the Deutsche Bank."

He lit the cigarette, took a deep puff, laid it in the ashtray, and leaned forward, his hands on his knees, and began talking in a low voice. "Our peasants were wise, were small landowners. We were the breadbasket of Europe. This nation fed the Deutsche army during World War II. Then came the Communists. The Communist dictators owned the country and behaved as if they were always there, before the mountains, before the sun, before the earth was created. The first generation were idealists, the second generation went abroad and wanted to become rich. And they discovered how to do it. They discovered corruption."

He sat back in his chair, sighed, and nodded his head as if savoring the full extent of their duplicity.

"And then came freedom. Communists disappeared. They turned into men who wanted to become rich. It was easy. They already knew corruption."

He shrugged, his hands held in front of him, palms up, while the cigarette smoke floated around him like a cloud.

"It's not a plot. There is no scenario. But what discipline they use. So smooth, the money disappears."

"Smuggled out of the country?" Chatham asked.

"Smuggling? That's the only way to make a living. But no one has reported even a single gram of drugs smuggled, not a single artifact." His eyes followed the smoke from his cigarette, pluming upward and toward the window. "In Bulgaria we have two moralities, a small morality and a big morality."

"Dual standards?"

"We don't have dual standards. We don't have any standards."

Dimitar fell silent, tipping the ash from his cigarette into the ashtray. He held the cigarette upright between his fingers and watched it burn. "We will come back from the ashes. Every house will be rebuilt stone by stone, man by man," he said, and stopped talking.

Chatham waited, his back straight against the chair, his hands in his lap.

"Your sister is very beautiful," he finally said into the silence.

"I know. We are the descendents of Thracians. They say the Thracians were handsome people. And the Thracian hoard, the one you saw on the train. That is also handsome. Is that why you came?"

Chatham didn't know how to answer. Certainly he couldn't say that he came to rescue Irena. Rescue her from what?

"I am, after all, an archaeologist," he said.

"Archaeologists, ach. I know about archaeologists. We have a tradition here in Bulgaria. We know archaeologists are fools."

Chatham bristled. "You mean the search for the Golden Fleece? For Jason and the Argonauts?" And for a moment Chatham wondered if the beautiful Irena was a descendant of the terrible Medea.

"No, no, worse than that," Dimitar said. "The brothers Schorpil were the first Bulgarian archaeologists. They searched the shattered walls of time to find our past and rescue it from the abyss of oblivion. But after that—ach. You know the story of the Cyclops?"

"From the *Odyssey*?"

"No. The Bulgarian Cyclops. An archaeologist hired some gypsies to help dig a tomb. They dug so fast, so hard, that a pick-axe went through a skull. Most of the skull was rotted away."

"Could be the tomb was in a limestone area," Chatham said. "Limestone leaches out the calcium from buried bone."

"Be that as it may, the pickaxe left a small hole in the middle of the forehead, and the archaeologist concluded that he had clear evidence of the existence of a Cyclops. He published a paper about it."

"Did anyone take it seriously?"

"A few years later, someone sent him a large package. Inside the package was another, and inside that yet another. And another and another, until at last he found a small box, like the kind they use for a jewel. Inside that was a fish scale and a note that said, 'Evidence of mermaids in the Black Sea.'"

Dimitar paused. Chatham knew he was expected to laugh, so he did.

Dimitar sighed and laid the cigarette in the ashtray, watching the smoke curl through the room as it burned down to ash.

"I see you like my sister. If you want to make a good impression on her, if you want to remain my friend, you will pay attention to the Thracian hoard."

So that was his game, Chatham thought. "You want me to buy it for the museum? I can't. Only the board of directors of the museum can make that decision."

"No, no," Dimitar said and moved uncomfortably in his chair.

Both men sat upright in their chairs, arms folded, waiting for the other to speak. Occasionally Dimitar nodded to himself, as if agreeing with some thought. At last, they heard a key in the lock.

"She's back," Dimitar said and went into the kitchen. Chatham listened to their muted voices punctuated by kitchen sounds—the clatter of plates, the scrape of drawers opening and closing. They emerged in a few minutes, balancing platters with bread, sliced cheese and sausage, tomatoes, roasted red peppers.

"Come, eat," Irena said and sat in the chair next to Chatham and put two pieces of bread on his plate. "Eat as you would at home."

"You are too hospitable," Chatham said with a slight bow.

Dimitar said, "Of course we are hospitable. We all say welcome, welcome with your money, dirty or not."

Irena gave her brother a sad smile. "Things could be worse." She sat with her arm extended, as if she were looking for something. "Wine," she said after a while. "I forgot the wine."

She pushed away from the table and went back to the kitchen. Chatham watched her, fascinated by the sensuous stride of her long legs, by the supple movement of her hips.

"Maybe we get help from America," Dimitar was saying. "Maybe NATO. I would like to see Bulgaria become a member of NATO."

Irena returned carrying a bottle of wine and three glasses. Chatham watched as her dress fell loosely from her shoulders when she bent over to pour the wine while Dimitar droned on.

"NATO is corrupt too, of course, but the right kind of corruption. I would like to see a new people finally—finally—come to oppress the Bulgarians instead of the Russians and Germans."

Irena lifted her glass. "It is not so bad. We have fine Bulgarian wine." She reached over and clinked glasses with Chatham. "To our friendship." She smiled at Chatham and leaned toward him when she put down her glass. "My brother is bitter. Things are hard here. You must excuse him."

"How do you make a living?" Chatham asked him.

Dimitar shrugged. "A little of this, a little of that."

"My brother is very good with his hands. He has a shop where he repairs clocks, and he has a dental laboratory. Neither does well, but between the two, we can keep food on the table."

"Thanks for my sister for that. We say in Bulgaria 'God provides the food, but he doesn't bring it into the house.'"

Irena pointed to the platter of food. "These are local special-ties, the roasted peppers, the salami." She put a few slices of salami on his plate. "Try it."

Chatham hated salami. It sat between his teeth, heavy with garlic and fat that clung to the roof of his mouth. He swallowed it almost whole and took a sip of wine to get rid of the taste.

"Delicious," he said and felt the lump of food stick in his gullet.

He tried to swallow once more and choked. Suddenly, he couldn't breathe, felt as if he were being strangled. He gasped for breath and the room began to dim and throb. He rested his head in his hands, waiting for the blackness and dizziness to pass.

"You all right?" Irena asked.

"It's nothing," Chatham rasped out in a whisper. "Went down the wrong channel."

"Take bread, take wine."

She filled his glass. He drank it down as if it were water and she filled it again.

Somehow, he got through the meal, watching Irena cut her sandwich into small portions, watching the movement of her lips as she chewed, savoring the delicious flick of her tongue as she licked her lower lip. He sipped from his glass whenever she lifted hers. All the while the seat of the ladder-back chair pressed into his leg and he was giddy with wine.

His eyelids began to droop and he yawned.

"You will stay," Irena said. She pointed to the faded sofa.

"You can study the Thracian hoard," her brother added, while visions of visits to the sofa from the beautiful Irena in the dark of night danced in Chatham's head.

"The Thracian gold," Chatham said. "I should study it, at the least I should draw it."

Dimitar nodded in agreement.

"And photograph it," Chatham said. "You have a camera?"

"No photographs. Too unsafe, someone will steal the gold."

Chatham wondered how photographs would be riskier than drawings, but said nothing. At least he could publish something, authenticate his find with drawings.

"I need to go to the stationer's," Chatham said. He had difficulty thinking. "Get some supplies."

"There's one not far from here," Irena told him. "On the other side of the cathedral. I'll take you."

Downstairs, the warm stillness of the summer air braced him like a tonic. They started toward the park, past tumbledown buildings with sagging roofs and chipped stucco.

"All other places in the world, you see building, buildings all going up," Irena said. "Here in Bulgaria, the buildings are all going down."

They had gone as far as the cathedral when two well-muscled men with short-cropped hair, wearing jeans and Oxford shirts, parked a Porsche at the curb.

Irena hesitated, took in her breath and grabbed his arm. "*Bortsi*!"

The men got out of the Porsche, slammed the door, crossed the square and ambled toward the park with a smooth, athletic gait.

She looked after them, still clinging to Chatham. He moved closer to her.

"*Bortsi* means wrestlers," she said.

"More brawn than brain?"

"They pretend to be body builders, ex-sportsmen."

She gripped his arm more firmly and Chatham felt the warm dampness of her body.

"Don't make them angry," she said. "Even the police are afraid of them."

At the stationer's, Chatham bought a pad of graph paper, India ink and pens, French curves and calipers, a protractor and a compass.

He found a Telex machine in an alcove in the back of the shop. He paid for a Telex to the British Museum telling them about the Thracian gold, said he would get in touch with them later, and asked them to send a message to Prague that he would be delayed.

For the next two days, he selected pieces from the treasure, measured and drew them, sitting at the table in a ladder-back chair until his back ached and his shoulders were sore. Occasionally, when Irena was near, he would get up to go to the kitchen for a glass of water, standing close to her, patting her arm, trying to edge closer. She would behave as if he weren't there, not moving, and give him a sideways glance and a smile.

In the evenings, he went out to the stationers and sent the day's notes about the hoard to the *Illustrated London News* by Telex.

Each night he dreamt of Irena. Each morning, he woke with a headache and a stiff neck. The sofa was hard, with missing springs, and the lumpy pillows smelled of mildew.

After two days, Dimitar came to him and said, "We have to talk," and told him to come to his shop.

He gave him the address on a piece of paper and told Chatham he expected him at one o'clock. Chatham took a taxi and gave the driver the address. They drove to a dingy street with empty shops, some with painted windows. Chatham found the number and opened the door.

He was surrounded by a cacophony of clocks, each ticking a different tock, each set at a different time, each banging out the hour, the half hour, the quarter to, from all four walls. Time assaulted him, with pendulums pitching in eternal arcs, with tinkling chimes and clanging tocsins, pushing one moment against the next with no chance of return.

Dimitar sat at a bench in a small room in the back of the shop, visible through an open door next to a grandfather clock that was proclaiming the hour.

"Come in, come in," Dimitar said. "You are in the right place."

He got up and moved slowly toward Chatham, eyeing him, nodding his head.

"Welcome to my shop." He leaned toward Chatham, his breath as rhythmic as the clocks and pungent with undigested food. "You see. You come when I call. You can't escape me." He stepped back and gestured at the clocks on the wall and paused, turning to look at them. "And you are running out of time."

Chapter Eight

Sofia, Bulgaria, August 9, 1990

"What do you want of me?" Chatham asked, raising his voice to speak over the din from the other room.

Another clock struck with a sonorous boom that quivered against the wall and shook small timepieces to attention. Dimitar seemed to be listening, counting. He pulled out a pocket watch, opened it, checked the time and nodded.

"You work at the British Museum?" Dimitar said at last in a deep rumble.

"I don't have the authority to buy anything on my own."

"No, no," Dimitar said.

"Purchases go through the Keeper of Near Eastern Studies." The discordant ticking from the next room beat at Chatham with a frantic rhythm. "It's a complicated process, takes time. The Keeper is the chief curator. He recommends the piece to the Director, who has it authenticated before it goes to the Board of Governors, which meets once a month." Chatham's words came faster and faster, in rhythm with the frantic ticking of the clocks. "I can send the drawings first. That's part of the reason I'm making them."

"I don't want to sell the gold to a museum."

"What do you want?"

"We need the money or we will starve."

"What then?"

"I read somewhere that when something is exhibited in a museum, it gains value."

"That's probably true."

"I want to sell the gold to private collectors. That way I get more money."

Chatham's tongue ran along his upper lip. "You want to take the collection to an auction house like Sotheby's? And you think that if you lend the Thracian Gold to the British Museum for a special exhibit, you can get more money when you sell it?"

"Exactly." Dimitar nodded. "We sell the gold after the exhibit."

"After the drawings are published in *The Illustrated London News*, there's a better chance that the museum will want to exhibit it."

"I give you a commission. The more money we get for the pieces, the more money you get."

Chatham thought about it, licked his lips and tried to calculate how much commission would he get. The collection would be worth millions if they handled it right.

Dimitar gave him a sharp look. "I see you like the money as much as you like my sister. More, perhaps."

"We need to know provenience." He felt he was speaking for the museum now.

"Provenance? It's been in my family for centuries."

"No, no. I know its been in your family, I know the provenance, the history of ownership. I mean where it originates archaeologically—provenience—the find spot. Can you take me where you found the gold?"

Dimitar gave him another penetrating look while he listened to the chime of yet another clock.

"Tomorrow," he said at last.

The three of them left Sofia early, at 6:30, after a hasty breakfast of pound cake and murky coffee. Dimitar pulled up in a dusty dark blue Mercedes with leather seats that were sticky with the heat.

Chatham raised his eyebrows.

"I got the car from a friend," Dimitar said.

They drove through towns with empty factories, their windows broken; through towns with houses with roofs that sagged beneath a scatter of broken tiles.

"This is all that's left," Dimitar said, watching Chatham's reaction. "Such is the fate and the evil of the crossroads. The Turks were wiser than the communists; they preserved the milk-cow. The communists cut off the head, destroyed the intelligentsia, and left the peasants."

Stop complaining, Chatham thought. They left you with the gold.

Beyond the villages, the road ran through undulating country with fields of grain, of sunflowers, of small grapevines marching in rows over hillocks and through valleys billowing with acres and acres of roses. Here and there, stands of lavender dotted the hillsides. And over all hung a sweet, heavy scent of roses.

They finally stopped at a farmhouse between a lavender field and a stand of trees on the edge of a wooded area. Dimitar parked the car behind a house next to a stable and riding ring. "There's no road from here. We need to go by horse."

He got out of the car and called to a man working in the field beyond the stable. The man turned, removed his large hat to wipe his forehead, then came toward them, rubbing at his hands, slapping them against his jeans, rubbing them again.

They spoke quietly, Dimitar gesturing in the direction of the woods. They disappeared into the stable and came out a few minutes later leading three saddled horses and brought them over to a small box on the ground near the riding ring.

Dimitar positioned a horse next to the box and turned to Chatham. "You know how to ride horses?"

He held the reins across the neck of a roan with a hefty rump and motioned for Chatham to mount.

Dimitar adjusted Chatham's stirrups. "You'll be all right?"

He held a creamy Palomino for Irena and helped her settle in the saddle, and mounted a small chestnut himself.

"Let's go," he said.

They rode along a path toward the woods at an easy lope for a while, until Dimitar made a clicking sound with his mouth and kicked his horse slightly, spurring it into a faster canter.

Irena followed. Her lips parted; her cheeks flushed; her shoulders moved in elegant repose at one with the horse, her back straight, as she sat astride the saddle, gripping it with her thighs. Chatham rode next to her and watched her, hair pulled back with a ribbon from her perfect face. He watched the ends of her hair streaming behind her, brushing against her cheek as she eased gently back and forth, back and forth, in rhythm with the canter. He watched her and watched her. This is what I want forever, he thought, to ride next to her and watch her, and he kicked his horse lightly with his heel and moved along beside her, back and forth, back and forth in the saddle.

They rode through the woods until they reached a chain-link fence topped with rolls of barbed wire.

"My own land, my patrimony, no longer mine," Dimitar said. "Fenced in and hidden from me." He gestured in the direction of a small mound.

"There it is, beyond the fence. I found the gold there, buried with an ancient Thracian horseman."

"You found it?"

"It was here to be found. My forefathers were horsemen. I was conceived among the horses. I am the guardian of all this, the guardian of time."

He dismounted and gripped the fence. "Our minds are naked without the past, exposed to the cold winds of time. Everything we know is preserved but is warped by fire and hatred."

"How did you find this place?"

"I told you, it's my own land. Was. My heritage rests in the rocks, hides among the horses. As a boy, in the night, I walked among the shadows of dead ruins and heard the beat of horses' hoofs in the distance. Each night I returned to that spot. Each night the horses came closer, until one night the horseman emerged from the darkness. And I followed."

"What happened?"

"The horse was not shod, so I knew. I knew the horseman was an ancient one. 'You know this place? You know what happened here?' he asked me. And then he told me, 'In the forest where no human voice had been heard, the ancient Getae came and built a sanctuary to the great God Zalmoxsis. Here they begged him for success in battle and sent a messenger, a brave warrior who had led in battle. He went over the cliff onto three sharp spears and they whispered their prayers while the spears still shone bright with his blood. They carried the warrior to the tomb, his drops of blood shining like rubies on the ground. From each drop grew a scarlet rose.'"

"Where did you hear this? There are texts?"

"I know. I just know. I heard it from the horseman." He shrugged and held out his hands. "Eternity rests in the rock and hides among the horses."

He walked back to his horse and remounted, pulling its head sharply in the direction of the farm where they had borrowed the horses. They ate under the trees at the farmhouse, a light lunch of bread and soup thickened with yogurt.

And then they drove back to Sofia, through the Valley of the Roses, through fields of roses burning scarlet in the sun.

Chapter Nine

Basel, Switzerland, August 9, 1990

Tamar took the airport bus from Mulhouse, the little airport in Alsace that serviced Basel, and checked into the Euler.

The desk clerk eyed her Indian gauze blouse and her jeans, her thick sandals. He pasted on a smile of mild disapproval. He asked for her passport and a credit card and looked pointedly at her dusty duffel bag while she rummaged through her purse.

Sedate ladies with pearls and portly businessmen in three-piece suits with gold watch-chains across their vests moved quietly through the staid lobby.

The clerk asked, "You'll be here how long?"

Tamar wasn't sure.

"A week," the desk clerk said when Tamar didn't answer. "Business or pleasure?" He rang for a porter and handed him the key. "Room 238. Elevators are around the corner to the right," he said without looking up from the registration form.

A bellboy picked up her bag and led her to the elevator. Upstairs, Tamar followed him down a long hall to a room near the service elevator and across the way from the pantry that the floor concierge used for morning coffee. The bellboy opened the door, handed Tamar the key, placed her battered bag on the luggage rack in the closet, opened the drapes, smiled, held out his hand, palm up, and said, "You are pleased with the room?" He waited. "Everything is all right?" he asked.

She scrambled through her purse and found a dollar bill. "Dollars okay? I haven't had time to stop at a bank."

His hand was still out. She gave him another dollar.

He looked over the bills and turned them in his hand as if they were counterfeit. "Bottled water is in the refrigerator bar." He gestured vaguely past the dresser, put the money in his pocket and edged into the hallway. "Call if you need something."

He left, closing the door behind him.

She examined the room: the wood-paneled walls; the antique armoire; the small refrigerator with a false wood front in the corner next to the dresser; the feather bed, puffy with the pristine downy white of the comforter and thick pillows.

She stared blankly at the walls and thought about the mosaic, about the last day at Tepe Hazarfen. Something wasn't right that day, even before she knew the mosaic was gone.

What was it? Something Mustafa said? Or was it earlier, was it Chatham?

Tired and thirsty, she rummaged in the refrigerator for a bottle of water and took a long draught before she fell on the bed and slept for an hour, dreaming of Alex again, as she always did.

This time, they were sipping iced tea on a terrace floating over an orange sea flecked with stars that blinked on and off, and Alex was saying to her over and over, "Be careful. It isn't what it seems. It isn't what it seems."

When she awoke, she checked herself in the mirror and fingered the amber beads against her blouse—heavy, dark, strung on a leather thong.

This will never do, she decided. I have to look rich, like I can afford to buy a mosaic floor. She had little in her suitcase besides clean underwear and two light cotton dresses that she saved for weekends. She had thrown away her torn digging clothes in Turkey, as she did every year.

She unpacked, found a terrycloth robe in the bathroom, found the soap and shampoo on the counter next to the sink, and climbed into the shower.

She selected a pale green knitted dress to wear. In Turkey it looked elegant when she wore it with the amber necklace. Here it looked shoddy and second-rate.

She shrugged, flung the strap of her clumsy leather purse over her shoulder, and went down to the concierge desk in the lobby. She asked for a city map, and asked the concierge to show her the main shopping street.

Another patronizing smile, this time from the concierge. The concierge opened the map and began to trace on it with a pen. "Here, between Barfüsserplatz and Marktplatz, you will find everything you need." She clicked the pen and looked Tamar over. "Shall I call you a cab?"

"It doesn't look as if it's that far. I'll walk."

The concierge looked down at Tamar's sandals and smiled again. "The taxi is complimentary."

"I want to get to know Basel."

"Suit yourself. Enjoy the lovely day." The concierge picked up the pen again poised it over the map. "When you leave the hotel, turn left, then right on this street." She made a mark on the map. "Then straight on. You can't miss the center of town."

Tamar wandered for the better part of half an hour, viewing the burghers of Basel with their dark suits and briefcases, and the grim-faced housewives wearing print dresses and colored shoes and waiting patiently at street corners for traffic lights to change.

No one smiled.

It's as though they have constipated souls, she thought, and went back to deciding what she had to buy. She had two credit cards, one for the hotel, one for clothes and other expenses. Shoes, she thought, shoes that match each outfit, like the ladies of Basel.

She passed a Bank Suisse and got two hundred dollars' worth of Swiss francs from the ATM machine. She looked up at the street sign and found herself at the corner of Aeschenvorstadt and Aeschenplatz. It can't be too far, she thought. She oriented herself on the map and found Barfüsserplatz.

She walked along Freiestrasse, looking in shop windows for appropriate clothes, taking short forays into side streets. She stopped outside a quiet shop with one dark outfit on a form in the window and peered inside. She saw a linen dress on a rack in the center of the shop, the kind of dress she needed, decided to look further, and continued on toward Marktplatz.

The Town Square, lined by corbelled houses, lay in the shadow of the Rathaus, the town hall, a red stone building adorned with frescoes and fluttering banners and topped by a multi-colored roof. Tamar navigated through a barricade of parked cars that edged the market in the center of the square.

She strolled through a cacophony of stalls that sold flowers, fruits, vegetables, bread, cheese, apples the color of the Rathaus, all under a sea of market umbrellas—white, yellow, fringed, scalloped. Pigeons cooed and bustled on the cobblestones below, pecking at bits of debris that had fluttered to the ground and lodged in little wet gutters between the stones.

She stopped at a fruit stand, drawn by the luscious scent of tiny wild strawberries, red and bright as the Rathaus.

"Picked fresh from the mountains," a woman in an apron who stood behind the table told Tamar in English.

In front was an array of yellow peaches with blushing cheeks, the tantalizing aroma of their sweet-acid tang wafting on the air.

"You want to buy?" asked the woman.

Tamar nodded and reached for a peach with a luscious crimson glow. Before she could, the woman placed it on the balance pan with two others, fiddled with brass weights on the platform of the scale until it was level, and shoveled the peaches into a paper sack.

Tamar made her way back to the shop where she had seen the dress. A bell attached to the top of the entrance tinkled when she opened it. The faint odor of a meal, of cooking meat, drifted from somewhere in the rear of the shop.

A woman in a dark blue smock came through the heavy drape that hung over the entrance to the back of the shop. She was still chewing. She swallowed, wiped her mouth with a napkin and put it in the pocket of her smock.

"I can help you?"

"I would like to see a dress."

The woman peered at Tamar and nodded her head. She took the napkin from her pocket and wiped at her mouth again. "You would like to see a dress?"

By the time Tamar left, she had bought three dresses. The last was a delicate aquamarine silk. "Just the color of your eyes," the saleswoman had said. "You have very good taste."

And now for shoes, Tamar decided. Shoe stores lined Freiestrasse, one after the other, all with Bally shoes. She found three pair to match the dresses, bought stockings, and a white straw purse with embroidered flowers.

Back at the Euler, Tamar assessed the spoils of her morning foray, hung the clothes in the closet, and lined up the shoes on the closet floor.

Shopping always tired her. She sat at the desk, stared at the drapes marching across the window in measured folds, wondering what she was doing here, how she could find the mosaic in the strangeness of Basel, and then roused herself to dress in her new finery and assail the lobby.

The manager stood near the revolving door talking to a stout matron when Tamar came around the corner from the elevator.

He raised his eyebrow in greeting, bowed to the stout lady and approached Tamar with a welcoming smile.

"Everything is to your satisfaction?" He reached out to shake her hand. "Charles Keller. Welcome to the Euler," he said with a vigorous shake of her hand.

He glanced toward the clock above the registration desk. "Cocktail time. Will you be my guest?" he asked and gestured in the direction of the bar.

They sat in low chairs at a black glass table in the dim light of the bar. Snatches of German words escaped from the murmur of voices of a man and woman at the far end of the room, soft piano music washed over the room from hidden speakers in the background. Tamar ordered a sherry.

A lighted glass showcase, a vitrine, behind the bar held some remarkable pieces of Greek pottery.

"The owner of the Euler is a collector?" Tamar asked.

"I am the owner." He gave Tamar a slight nod of the head. "And the manager. And a collector."

"The pieces in the vitrine are real?"

"Real pottery, not real antiquities. Just very good copies. I once displayed real pieces here, but now in a public place, even here at the Euler...." He held out his hands, palms up and shrugged, "It is not a very good idea."

"But you collect?"

"Everyone in Basel is a bit of a collector. Here in Basel, we have a fine *Antikenmuseum*. It inspires people to collect."

"There must be a number of good antiquities dealers in Basel."

"Of course. There is a fancy shop for tourists near the Art Museum. There is a famous art dealer on Engelstrasse. He acquired most of the collection for Dumbarton Oaks, specializes in Turkish material. He's retired now, writing a corpus of ancient Byzantine coins. You can only see him by appointment." He contemplated the vitrine with the pottery for a moment. "The best one," he said, "the most reliable dealer with the best pieces, is Gilberto Dela Barcolo. He's on Hohenstrasse, in one of the patrician houses off Engelgasse south of Saint Alban district."

He looked over Tamar's shoulder as someone approached the table and he rose to hold out his hand in greeting.

She turned to see a bronzed, compact man with gray smoky eyes.

"Ah. Enzio," the manager said. "Good to see you back." He turned to Tamar and indicated the man who had just joined them. "Enzio Egidio."

Enzio acknowledged the introduction with a slight bow. "At your service. And your name?"

"Tamar Saticoy."

"American?"

"From California."

Someone in the lobby caught Keller's eye. "You will excuse me?" he said, and left them in the bar.

"You want a Campari?" Enzio asked Tamar. His hands were perched on the back of her chair.

"No, I don't."

"You flew ten thousand miles and clear across the sea. You need something to soothe the aches and pains of outrageous fortune," he said, and sat down.

She raised an eyebrow.

"I quote from Guglielmo Shakespeare, the famous Italian poet and playwright," he said.

"You're Italian?"

"From Napoli."

A waiter in black pants and a white shirt came to their table and stood next to Enzio with a pencil poised over a pad. "*Prego?*"

Tamar ordered a bottle of Evian water.

"And a Campari for me."

Tamar made a face. "Tastes medicinal."

"I need it for your sake. You must be exhausted."

"How sympathetic."

"*Simpatico* is the word."

"And brash."

"That too."

He was trying to be bright and witty, and not quite making it. Tamar felt embarrassed for him. She wanted to say, relax, be yourself, but contemplated him instead in comfortable silence.

He reached into his pocket and took out a packet of American cigarettes, Marlboros, and offered her one. She shook her head.

"No vices at all?" he asked and fiddled with the cigarette.

The waiter brought their drinks, set the water bottle and a glass in front of Tamar and poured some water into it.

"What are you doing in Basel?" Enzio asked.

Tamar sipped from her glass. "I came for the waters." She put down the glass and made a circle with her fingers with the drops of water on the table. "I collect antiquities. I came to shop."

"That's a rich man's game." He seemed more at ease now, and leaned back in his chair. "You're not rich."

"You don't know that."

"You can always tell by the shoes."

She moved her feet farther under the table.

"You're wearing Ballys bought locally, not the kind for export."

"I'm buying antiquities for my museum."

"You're a curator?"

"A university professor. Archaeologist."

He looked skeptical. "Archaeologists don't buy antiquities. I heard that it's against their principles."

"Usually. We had a windfall, a donor who gave us money to start a museum, and he wants it to open with some major pieces."

"All with the proper provenance, of course."

Tamar waved the word away with her hand. "Provenance is an art historian's term."

"And you don't approve of art historians?"

"They only care about artifacts as *objets d'arte*, all out of context, all without meaning. As far as they are concerned, authentication comes from a list of previous owners—provenance."

"And how do you decide about authenticity?"

"From provenience, from the find spot, the site and the location within the site. I want to know what place the artifact had in the life of those who used it, who touched it, who saw it. I want to feel the same awe that they felt when they held it."

"Then why are you here?"

"I told you, for the museum. You seem to know something about the antiquities trade. You're a collector?"

"Not exactly. Sometimes."

"You don't look very rich either."

He lifted his foot. "Brunos," he said with a flourish toward his shoe.

"Who's Bruno? An antiquities dealer?"

"A shoe manufacturer. You never heard of Bruno Magli?"

"I'm looking for antiquities, not shoes. I don't know where to start." She waited for him to make a suggestion. "You know any antiquities dealers?" she finally asked.

"Try Gilberto Dela Barcolo. Ask anyone about him. He's the prince of dealers, the Duveen of the antiquities trade."

"Duveen was a bit of a scoundrel."

Enzio took a sip of his Campari and made a face. "Exactly," he said.

"Everything from this Dela Barcolo has provenience?"

"Provenance. If it doesn't have one, he'll get one for you."

She looked down at his shoes. "He wears Brunos?"

He nodded.

Gilberto Dela Barcolo it is, Tamar decided. I'll try there in the morning.

She took a sip of water. "Who are you?" she asked him. "Besides Enzio from Napoli who wears the right kind of shoes."

"A man with proper provenance." He contemplated his foot and moved it from side to side. "I have to visit Gilberto tomorrow. I can take you there, if you want to come along."

She hesitated, then decided that she would rather go on her own. She reached for the water bottle to take up to her room. "I have to go now."

He stood up when she did and threw twenty francs on the table. "Tomorrow, here, at eleven?"

"Don't wait," she said.

Chapter Ten

Basel, Switzerland, August 10, 1990

At ten thirty in the morning, Tamar took a cab to Gilberto Dela Barcolo's house in the St. Alban's district. Herr Keller, the manager at the Euler, had given her the address and called for an appointment.

"It's his home," Herr Keller told her. "Full of beautiful antiquities. He loves beautiful things, lives with them, sits back and admires them. You'll see."

"*Hohenstrasse Sieben,*" she told the taxi driver in her best German and leaned back in the seat.

"*Hohnstrosse Siebe,*" the driver corrected her in Basler *Schwyzertuesch*. He nodded to himself and then nodded to her in the rear view mirror before he started the meter and drove off.

Hohenstrasse was a narrow, quiet street crammed with staid cars, mostly gray Mercedes, and lined with upscale nineteenth century townhouses. The taxi stopped before the largest of these, a three story stone house behind an elaborate wrought iron gate.

The driver printed a chit from the meter, handed it to her, and grunted. She counted out the fare and tip.

"*Merci viel mals,*" the driver said in the local patois, and Tamar smiled at the mixture of French and German.

She stood in the street for a moment, then opened the gate that went along the path between low rose hedges. Halfway up the walk, she stopped. Her heart thumped and her hands grew clammy, with a chill of trepidation, beset with worry about meeting a stranger, about finding the mosaic.

She took a deep breath and continued up the walk, up the steps to the door, and rang the bell. She waited and peered through the beveled glass into a short vestibule with five marble steps covered by a red carpet anchored with brass rods. All seemed silent inside the house.

A second pair of double doors stood closed at the top of the stairs. She pressed the bell again and heard the echo of a harsh ring reverberate in the foyer beyond.

A man wearing a dark turtleneck sweater and fine Italian shoes opened both doors at the top of the stairs with a flamboyant gesture. He was strikingly handsome, with liquid brown eyes caught in thought and dark hair tumbling onto his forehead. He frowned, holding a finger to his lips, and ducked his head to see who rang the bell. When he saw Tamar waiting, he came striding down the red carpet with easy grace.

He opened the door with a flourish and held out his hand. "Gilberto Dela Barcolo. Sorry you had to wait, Miss Saticoy. The housekeeper seems to have gone off somewhere."

He waved her in with a slight bow. "You are Miss Saticoy, aren't you?"

His hair had a touch of gray at the temples, just enough to make him distinguished.

He reached for her hand and gave it an air kiss. "Please to come in."

Everything about him was suave and sleek and charming, even his voice, so mellifluous and resonant with a faint Italian accent.

They climbed the stairs into a grand foyer. A domed skylight high above a patterned mosaic in the center of the floor immersed it in a luminous twilight. At the far wall, a staircase led up to a second floor gallery, and then a third. A fine antique Oriental rug, the colors muted by time, hung on the wall behind the landing. The far corner of the gallery held a desk and another glass showcase.

Dela Barcolo made a casual gesture in the direction of the carpet. "A Shah Abbas," he said with a modest smile.

He climbed the stairs to the landing, quiet elegance permeating every move, and stood in front of the carpet, waiting for her to follow.

He turned back the corner of the carpet to show the fine quality of the stitches. "You know about Shah Abbas," he said. "Shah Abbas the Great. He ruled Persia in the sixteenth century and was renowned for his conquests, his cruelty, and the magnificence of his court, the buildings he erected, and the beauty of their furnishings. Especially the carpets."

"Very nice," Tamar said.

"But you want something older, something ancient, something wrapped in the romance of a more distant past," he said and they continued up the stairs to the gallery.

A marquetry desk and chair and the head and shoulders of a Kore, larger than life, on a high black acrylic plinth were in the far corner near the railing of the gallery.

The nose and right ear had been repaired, conservator style, with plaster painted the same gray color as the stone.

A vitrine stood against the back wall.

As they walked toward it, the pressure of their steps along the gallery seemed to rock the Kore on the plinth. Tamar reached up to steady it.

"Careful," Dela Barcolo said. "It isn't permanently installed. For that we have to drill a hole. It's a Kore—the Maiden, Persephone, Queen of the Underworld. Her statue, garlanded with flowers during the celebration of the Elysian Mysteries, stood in a temple dedicated to the Kore and her mother Demeter. Perhaps you're interested?"

Tamar shook her head. "Not what I was looking for."

"No?" Dela Barcolo crossed over to the vitrine and reached inside. "I have something special," he said. "A Kybele."

"A Kybele?"

Like the one stolen from Ephesus?

He brought out a ceramic figurine of a Roman matron wearing a chiton and himation and enthroned on a wheeled chariot. She wore the attributes of Kybele, a polis headdress and lions on either side of the throne.

"That's Kybele?" Tamar asked.

Dela Barcolo laughed. "You were expecting the terrible Anatolian Kybele, of the castrated priests?" He moved to the desk, placed the figurine carefully on top and stood back. "This is the Roman version of the Mother Goddess, the Magna Mater, the Great Mother of the Gods. Like a good Italian mother, she is a nurturer. She probably cooks for her children."

He laughed again. "Originally, the Roman Kybele was a meteor that had fallen from the sky somewhere in Asia Minor, near Pergamum. They anointed it with oil and draped it with garlands and wreaths to consecrate the rock."

He stroked the figurine gently. "Beautiful, isn't she? When the Romans were fighting Hannibal, the Sybil told them they could only conquer Carthage if the Kybele were brought to Rome from Pergamum. The goddess was formally welcomed in Rome and placed in the pantheon to become, eventually, the principal goddess, known to Romans as the Great Mother of the Gods. During her festival, her worshippers anointed and dressed her and paraded her through the streets in a chariot drawn by two lions. In time, her cult was rivaled only by the cults of Isis and Mithras."

He reached into the top drawer of the desk, pulled out a yellowed envelope and extracted a letter, worn thin at the folds. "The piece has impeccable provenance." He pointed to the crest on the letterhead. "It was part of the collection of the Marquis de Cuvier."

Everything from Dela Barcolo has provenance, if not, he'll get one for you, Enzio had told her.

"Very nice," Tamar said.

"Some people see a relationship between Kybele and the Black Stone of the Kaaba in Mecca. The Black Stone, too, is a meteorite." He shrugged. "Scientists tell us that life may have been carried to Earth on the crust of a meteor. Who knows? Perhaps a meteorite is the mother of us all."

She waited a moment and then said, "I would be interested in something a little more..."

"Sensational," he said.

He refolded the letter from the Marquis de Cuvier and put it away in the desk, carried the Kybele with both hands back to its shelf and started back down the stairs.

He led her to two glass cases attached to the wall in the vestibule and filled with a range of eclectic artifacts: Roman glass vials, Mesopotamian clay statuettes of bearded worshippers with clasped hands and sheepskin skirts, Astarte figures with coffee bean eyes and elaborate headdresses, bronze figurines from Sardinia that looked like little robots.

He reached into one case and took out a larger clay statuette of a clean-shaven man in a robe, wearing what looked like a cap with a wide headband.

"Gudea, the ancient king of Lagash in Sumeria," he said, running his finger along the folds of the robe. "Is it not beautiful?"

"I was thinking of something larger, more impressive for the public."

"You're buying for a museum?"

She nodded. "A university museum." How could she put it, so that he wouldn't suspect that she was seeking a stolen mosaic? "Something Roman perhaps, something grand that we could put at the entrance to catch the eye of visitors."

"Which university?"

"California State."

"Ah, the University of California. I know the institution."

She began to say no, they are not the same, and then thought better of it. Too complicated to explain. Besides, she wasn't going to buy anything anyway. "Yes," she said and followed him into a sitting room.

Tamar navigated around a coffee table and between two settees toward a stele fragment set on an easel next to the fireplace.

"From the palace at Nineveh," Dela Barcolo said. "It belongs in a museum. You see here?" His finger traced a multitude of mounds incised on the stele. "The mountains. And here," indicating a cluster of wavy lines, "a river. You see the soldiers, who came down from the mountains and crossed the river?" He pointed to a line of armored men wearing pointed helmets and carrying spears.

The stone was dark and cracked. "It looks burnt," Tamar said.

"Of course, of course, the palace was destroyed by the invading Medes…"

The sharp jangle of the doorbell interrupted him. Dela Barcolo looked toward the back of the house, waited a moment until the bell rang again.

He sighed. "The housekeeper is still out. Please to excuse me."

He disappeared into the vestibule. Tamar examined the stele again. The same style as the ones at the British Museum depicting Sennacherib's conquest of Lachish, except that those at the British Museum don't have as much evidence of burning. This may be part of the same series, she thought, and wondered how Dela Barcolo got it, whom he had bribed, how many crimes had been committed on the way to acquiring it.

She shrugged. One man's Mede is another man's Persian, she thought, and moved to the window to look out. Enzio stood at the entrance. Behind him, a taxi pulled up. A woman with bleached and pampered hair and shoe-button eyes emerged, carrying packages with both arms, and darted up the walk past Enzio. Tamar heard a tumble of rapid Italian coming from the foyer hall and saw the woman storm toward the back of the house, shaking her head.

Enzio stood in the doorway of the living room, leaning against the jamb, smiling at her, almost laughing.

"I took your advice," he said to Tamar. "I didn't wait."

"You know each other?" Dela Barcolo asked, looking from one to the other.

"We met at the hotel," Tamar said.

Dela Barcolo moved closer to Tamar and blocked her view of Enzio. "You are stopping at the Euler?"

She nodded.

"You will stay for lunch?"

"Of course she will," Enzio said. "Your lunches are famous."

"And you," he said to Enzio. "You'll stay for lunch."

"Not today." Enzio looked at his watch. "I can only stay a few minutes. I have an appointment with Aristides at one."

Dela Barcolo bristled. "You brought something to sell? You offer it to Aristides before you show it to me?"

"I'm not showing it to Aristides. I'll bring it here tomorrow."

"Then stay for lunch."

"I can't."

Dela Barcolo shrugged and threw up his hands. "Fabiana!" he called, and made his way to the back of the house.

Enzio stood in front of the stele from Nineveh, and examined it while Tamar wandered the room. She stopped before one of two small curio tables with glass tops and velvet lined trays that held golden earrings shaped like ram's heads, intaglios set into rings, brooches with the dull yellow luster of ancient gold.

Enzio continued to peer at the stele, running his fingers along the surface. "I wonder where he got this."

"I've been wondering too," Tamar said.

"He just acquired it. It's been around for a while. The site was dug in the thirties."

"You know a lot about archaeology, don't you?" Tamar said.

"Of course he does," Dela Barcolo said in his smooth voice as he burst into the room.

"My housekeeper," he said. "She was at the police, giving a deposition. Two weeks ago, we were robbed. We had a flood in the basement when the washing machine overflowed. Fabiana left a window open to dry it out and the thief crawled in through the basement window. Somehow, he got into the safe and stole a collection of rare ancient coins. The police recovered the coins and are holding him." He gave Tamar a slight bow. "You will excuse me while I call to ask about the trial date."

He went into a small alcove off the living room, opened a polished mahogany box on the table, took out a telephone and punched numbers into the keypad inside the box. He spoke into the telephone, listened for a moment, then slammed down the receiver.

"They released him!"

"After Fabiana's deposition?" Enzio said.

Dela Barcolo held out his hands in a gesture of frustration. "They say they refuse to get involved in my sordid household intrigues."

"The thief is a friend of Fabiana's?" Enzio asked.

"She knows him. Mario started as one of my runners. He became a minor dealer, tries to sell me small Etruscan vases, Bucchero ware sometimes. Nothing important." He smiled and shook his head and threw up his hands in a dramatic gesture. "And now, he's a special friend of Fabiana's."

"He stole only the coins?"

"Thanks to God, he didn't take more."

Enzio raised his eyebrows and gave Dela Barcolo a knowing nod. "And he knew when the window to the basement was open, and somehow found the hiding place of the safe and figured out the combination."

"What are you saying, Enzio? All this can be explained."

"By Fabiana? It's up to you, Gilberto. It's your house she lives in."

Fabiana came into the room, set a tray of drinks down on the table in front of the fireplace, and flounced out.

"You think she heard you?" Gilberto asked.

"No," Fabiana called from the dining room. "I was in the chicken."

"Kitchen," Enzio said.

Gilberto picked up one of the glasses. "Leave her alone. Have a Bloody Mary. Good for your soul."

He strolled over to one of the small glass-topped curio tables on the other side of the room.

"You like jewelry?" he asked Tamar. "Something for yourself, for you to wear, perhaps? Something precious to grace your beauty, something worn long ago by another beautiful woman."

Tamar bent over the table. "Nothing for me, thank you. Just for the museum. But if I did…" She pointed, not to the jewelry, but to one of two small, carved stone figures shaped like a violin, an abstract representation of a woman common in Neolithic sites in the eastern Mediterranean.

"Of course," Dela Barcolo said. "A goddess. How fitting for you to choose her. You are a goddess yourself."

Tamar took a step away from the table.

"Friends call me Gilberto. And your friends call you?"

"Tamar."

"Tamar it is, then. May I call you Tamar?"

Enzio beamed at them and said, "I have to go now and leave you two to your own devices," as Fabiana called from the dining room that lunch was ready. "I can find my way out."

The large table was set for two with lace placemats, polished silver, Baccarat glasses, and a small pink rose next to each plate. *Cecile Brunner*, Tamar thought, remembering the tumble of climbing roses in her grandmother's garden, where each rosebush had a name and a lineage.

The lunch began with ox-tail soup, spiced with a little Scotch, then came Coquille St. Jacques.

At the head of the table, Gilberto Dela Barcolo presided like a king dispensing favors. He exuded charm like syrup, from the tips of his graceful fingers, from his dark Italian eyes, from his charismatic smile.

Between courses, she thought she detected a movement of his right leg searching for a floor-button. Each time he moved his leg, Fabiana would appear a few seconds later to clear the empty plates and bring on the next dish, just as Tamar's grandmother summoned the maid from the kitchen with her little glass bell.

For a moment, Tamar was a child again, caught in her grandmother's stern admonitions. Keep your elbows off the table. Close your mouth when you chew. No singing at meals.

Always a spectator, always kept at arm's length, stinging with her grandmother's resentment through the haunting loneliness, never to see her brothers again.

She found solace only in the past, traveled the world in search of herself, of the memory of her lost brothers, of her lost mother and father. Always a wanderer, always a stranger. Until with Alex she was safe at last, asleep in the hollow of his arm, comfortable enclosed in his affection.

"My family is from Venezia," Gilberto was saying as Tamar looked down at the table.

The plate was Wedgwood, the dish was veal piccata, and it tasted like ashes.

He patted the bottle of wine and turned the label toward Tamar. "Our coat of arms." He pointed to the small red shield near the bottom of the label depicting a diminutive sailboat floating on a lake with a castle in the background. "We have a small estate in the hills in the Piedmont where I spent the summers of my childhood." He tapped the image of the boat on the label with his fork, his eyes dark and soulful, his smile slick and elegant. "Our name means 'little boat' in Italian. Viscount Dela Barcolo." He shrugged. "Of course, we no longer use the title."

They had just finished dessert when Gilberto stretched his leg again. It seemed to be his left leg this time, searching for another button on the floor. Two wall panels facing Tamar opened. Tamar's mouth dropped in astonishment as she watched the silent panels move as if by a magician's wand. Behind them, on mirrored shelves lit from above and behind, was a marvel of artfully arranged Classical Greek pottery—Geometric, Corinthian, black on red, red on black—each resting on a Plexiglas display stand.

"Lovely, isn't it?" Gilberto said, gesturing toward the open cabinets.

He rose from his chair and stood in front of one of the cupboards. "You will like this." He waved her over. "Come. I'll show you magnificent things."

He took a *kylix*, a graceful, shallow cup on a pedestal base with horizontal handles, from its stand and held it carefully in his hands. The cup was smooth black, with palmettes and draped red figures painted around the outside of the rim.

"You want something like this, perhaps." He turned it over. "You see here." He pointed to the Greek lettering on the base. "It is signed. Epiktetus." He turned it back to show her the inside of the *kylix*. "And here, in the tondo." He pointed to the circle in the center. "A flute player and dancer."

"Beautiful," she said.

He looked at her and leaned closer. "Not half so beautiful as you."

"Is that how you always begin?"

He shook his head and moved closer still. "You hold me with your eyes. Your eyes are magic."

She backed away. "I've heard many a line, but none this smooth." He was so charming, so good looking that she almost forgave him. "You're a great salesman."

"Indeed I am." He bent over, his mouth close to her ear, and said in a throaty whisper, "And I'm going to sell you my soul."

I'd rather you offered me a mosaic, she thought, but later, in the cab on the way back to the Euler, all she thought about was what Gilberto said and the way he had said it, not wanting to feel the slight pleasure it gave her.

That evening when Tamar stopped in the bar for a bottle of water before she went upstairs, she saw Enzio seated at a table in the far corner. He waved her over and she sat down.

"What do you think of Gilberto?"

"He has quite a line."

"Be careful," Enzio told her. "You'll get caught in it and he'll reel you in."

Chapter Eleven

Sofia, Bulgaria, August 11, 1990

Chatham enclosed a note advising that there was more to follow with the packet of drawings that he mailed to the *Illustrated London News*.

Irena had gone to the post office with him. "You will go to London now?" she asked.

She stopped to buy a newspaper at the kiosk outside the post office as they made their way back to the small apartment on Ulitza Rakovsky. The street was misty, the sky overcast.

"I have more drawings to do," he told her.

"You could take the gold with you."

"The gold isn't what bothers me," Chatham said.

"What then?"

"I want to spend more time on the drawings," he said. And linger close to Irena with restless dreams of reaching for her in the night on the lumpy bed in Ulitza Rakovsky. "Would you miss me?"

"Certainly."

He thought of the triumph of marching into the British Museum bearing his find of the Thracian hoard.

"I'll come back."

"With the gold," she said. "When the exhibition is finished."

Chatham felt a chill of apprehension. He didn't know why. Maybe it was the way she said it, moving away from him as she spoke.

"I'll call for a plane reservation," she said.

"Today?"

"When we get back to the apartment."

It began to rain and they hurried through the wet streets, past *bortsi* standing on street corners who followed them with their eyes. Chatham reached for Irena to put his arm protectively across her shoulder, but she was steps ahead of him, running through the rain with the newspaper over her head.

"It will be safe?" Irena asked after Chatham made a plane reservation for five o'clock that afternoon.

"Not to worry. We will insure the gold," Dimitar said.

"The museum will insure it," Chatham told him.

"They will? They will pay the insurance, the whole cost?"

"Of course," Chatham said.

Dimitar nodded his head in satisfaction. "That is good." He clapped Chatham on the shoulder with a smile. "Go now. We pack the gold while you make the arrangements."

Chatham walked back through the rain with a borrowed raincoat and umbrella to the travel agent across from the stationer's, and passed more *bortsi* who skulked in doorways to keep out of the rain. He paid for the plane ticket with a credit card that Emma didn't know about, and crossed the street to the stationers. He sent a Telex to the Keeper of Near East Antiquities at the British Museum, telling him that he was bringing a collection of Thracian gold on loan for a possible exhibit.

He knew the museum couldn't arrange for insurance until the collection was authenticated and evaluated. It didn't matter. He wouldn't let go of it until he reached Heathrow, wouldn't let it out of his sight until it was safely deposited in the museum. Now that he could take it with him, he would have time to do the research, have the pieces photographed and tested.

He showed Irena the ticket when he returned. She held it in her hand for a moment, then gave it back.

"You must hurry." She flicked an imaginary piece of lint from his lapel. "You will be safe?"

"Not to worry. The gold is insured," Dimitar told her. He turned to Chatham. "It is, yes?"

"As of twenty minutes ago," Chatham said without a blink. "By Lloyd's, the best."

Irena nodded. "Lloyd's. I've heard of them." She kissed his cheek and reached for the telephone. "You must go now. The sooner you go, the sooner you come back. The plane leaves soon. I'll call for a cab." She dialed a number and said something in Bulgarian. She seemed angered with whatever she heard, then gave a disgusted shrug and slammed down the receiver. "The phone doesn't work." She held her finger against her lips a moment, as if she were thinking.

"There's always a line of taxis near the Cathedral of Alexander Nevsky," Dimitar said. "The rain has stopped now. You could cut through the park to the Cathedral."

He missed the look passed between Irena and Dimitar. "Why is he *Saint* Alexander Nevsky?" he asked.

Dimitar shrugged. "He was a great hero. He defeated the Swedes and the Germans and saved the Slavs from the west."

"I always thought that saints were either anorexic women or schizophrenics who thought they talked to God," Chatham said.

"Oh, Andrew, you are incorrigible," Irena said. Then she laughed and kissed Chatham on the other cheek and he felt strong and invulnerable.

"You will be safe going through the park?"

"I can handle it," he said.

"Dimitar can go with you," she said.

"I have to wait here for a call from a client," Dimitar said. "Then we can go."

"He'll miss the plane," Irena said.

"I'll miss the plane," Chatham said

Irena straightened his tie and smoothed his lapel. "I will miss you," she said, and moved him toward the door. "Go quickly. The sooner you go, the sooner you come back."

He picked up the suitcase and felt the heft of it tug at his arm. He moved toward Irena and bent to kiss her goodbye, but she had already turned away. His cheek brushed the back of her shoulder and he kissed the empty air.

"You must hurry," she said from the door of the kitchen. "The plane leaves in less than two hours."

Chatham hastened along the path through the park, the weight of the suitcase dragging at his shoulder. He still felt the warmth of Irena's earlier kiss on his cheek.

Wet leaves and buds lay on the damp earth. The park seemed to come alive, basking in the cool sparkle after a rain. Pigeons pecked at the ground at the edge of puddles left by the rain; twigs snapped in the bushes along the path where dogs prowled and foraged for food.

In front of Chatham, a bulky man, muscles bulging in his tight T-shirt, strolled aimlessly in the dappled light toward the cathedral.

A *bortsi*, Chatham thought, and slowed his pace.

His shoulder began to ache from the weight of the suitcase.

As Chatham slowed, the man in front of him seemed to hesitate.

Footsteps sounded from behind. Chatham turned to see another *bortsi* bearing down on him. Chatham hurried along the path. The suitcase banged against his leg and the sounds all around him seemed to be magnified—footsteps behind him quickening, moving in on him, bushes beside the path crackling with snarling dogs fighting for scraps.

The *bortsi* behind him seemed to speed up. I must be imagining it, Chatham thought. Irena wouldn't do that.

The man in front stopped, hands on hips, arms bent at the elbow, and blocked the path. He turned to face Chatham, powerful legs spread, smiling, arms open as if in welcome, while from behind the footsteps accelerated, closer, closer.

Dimitar, that's who it must be, Dimitar did this.

Just for a moment, heart thumping, Chatham hesitated, then took his chances with the feral dogs. He ducked into the bushes, swinging the suitcase in a wild arc at the man blocking the path as he went. The man went down with a soft whimper of surprise.

The dogs bayed at Chatham. One gripped his ankle. He felt a sharp pain and tried kicking at the dog. He swung the suitcase again, this time at the dog. It fell back with a yelp. Chatham careened out of the bushes, his heel landing on the *bortsi* in front of him, still splayed on the path. Chatham kicked him, heard the man groan. He swung the suitcase again, this time behind him. He felt the impact, heard a contact thump, then a grunt and a moan.

The man in front struggled to rise. Holding the suitcase out at arm's length, Chatham flayed in wide arcs, banged against the temple of the man in front, swung at the *bortsi* behind. Without looking to see what happened, Chatham sprinted out of the park, gripping the suitcase to his chest, his breath coming in agonized puffs, listening for the sound of pursuit.

He reached the bank of taxis and started toward the first in the rank. No, Dimitar may have set that one up in case he got away from the *bortsi* in the park. Not the second one, too obvious.

The driver of the third taxi in the rank opened the door and Chatham jumped in and fell onto the back seat.

"Lock the doors," he ordered.

The driver reached for the button on the panel next to him and all four doors locked with a satisfying snap. Outside, the drivers of the first two taxis shouted and shook their fists at Chatham.

"The airport. Hurry," Chatham said.

The driver turned to look over his shoulder as he backed up and Chatham recognized his steely eyes and his scar.

"I know you," Chatham said. "You're the driver who brought me to Ulitza Rakovsky."

The driver maneuvered the taxi out of the parking space and started away from the square. Chatham contemplated the back of the driver's head.

"You owe me ten leva," the driver said.

Black and gray hairs stood out on rolls and folds of fat below the cap on the back of the driver's head.

"I'll pay you. Just get me to the airport on time."

The taxi snaked in and out of traffic, along broad boulevards lined with square apartment blocks.

Chatham's leg began to throb. He looked down and noticed that his cuff was torn and his ankle was bleeding.

"You cheated me," the driver said.

"Don't worry. I'll pay you," Chatham told him.

The traffic was lighter now, and the taxi accelerated. The blocks of apartments were thinning out.

"This isn't the way to the airport," Chatham said.

His ankle was getting more painful.

"Take me to the airport." He took ten leva from his pocket and tossed it on the seat in front of him. "Here's your ten leva."

The cab speeded up.

Chatham reached into his pocket again and threw ten more leva on the seat. "Here's twenty."

They passed villas with broken balconies and sagging roofs, speeding faster and faster as they went.

"Stop the car," Chatham yelled at the back of the driver's implacable head.

He tried to open the door and remembered that the panel next to the driver controlled the locks. Damn Dimitar.

"I'll pay you double to get me to the airport."

In his peripheral vision, he saw scattered villas fly by the window and realized they were nearing the outskirts of town.

"You're going the wrong way."

Soon they would approach open country.

"This isn't the way to the airport," he shouted to the back of the driver and the car continued to race relentlessly in the wrong direction.

Chapter Twelve

Basel, Switzerland, August 12, 1990

Tamar opened her eyes, stretched luxuriously in the featherbed, put on the terry robe that the hotel provided, and rang for the floor concierge to bring breakfast—filtered coffee, butter, a basket of croissants, and small pots of jam. She opened the door a crack and retrieved the shoes she had left out the night before. They always reappeared in the morning, shining and tidy, lined up next to the door. She looked for the newspaper and then remembered it was Sunday. She felt slightly annoyed at the inconvenience, then laughed at her reaction.

I'm an archaeologist, she thought, why am I complaining? I dig in the dirt with a cramp in my knee and dust in my hair. I couldn't live without it, the adventure of it, the thrill of handling the artistry of long dead hands, the chance to whisper to the past.

When she first came to dig at Tepe Hazarfen, the dig house in Kilis was so bad that when she told the driver, "The mansion of Neshet Effendi," he stopped at the police station to pick up a gendarme, sure that the address was a mistake. When they found it, the house had broken windows, peeling paint, and Orman's head popping over the cracked garden wall like a jack-in-the-box on a spring.

He called out, "Tamar, is that you?" as the car drove up.

The garden was filled with trash, old tires and broken bottles, the detritus of abandonment since the turn of the century when it was last occupied. Nights, Orman and Chatham crashed through the house with a broom chasing bats, turning lights on and off because Chatham had said bats go toward the light.

"What do you mean, go toward the light?" Orman would say. "They're bats, you damned fool, they're blind. Blind as bats."

But here at the Euler, with her featherbed and her morning luxuries, she delighted in opulence. This is the life, she decided, this is how I will live from now on, surrounded by servants and comfort. She stretched again, amused at the prospect.

She foraged in the small refrigerator in the corner of the room for the last peach she had bought at Marktplatz then opened the door at the knock of the floor concierge. He carried the tray to the small table near the windows and she gave him a five-franc note. He closed the door gently as he left.

She yawned again luxuriously before she turned on the television and began surfing through the channels, looking for a program in English. She passed a station, mostly static and snow, with an image that wavered in and out, and thought she recognized a picture of Chatham.

Why Chatham?

She turned up the volume. Some incomprehensible words filtered through the interference in a Slavic language. Czech, maybe? Some Cyrillic letters appeared below the picture, and then it faded out. She shrugged, went on surfing hoping to find a broadcast from the BBC. She gave up, settled on a foggy French station with a wavering performance of *Les Sylphides*, and sat down to breakfast.

She had almost finished when the door buzzer sounded. She looked through the peephole to see Gilberto's head, nodding in rhythm to some inner music.

Tamar opened the door and he sailed in, carrying three large shopping bags filled to the brim and bright with flowers cut off at the stem: asters the color of jewels, dainty rosebuds, yellow daisies, white daisies, zinnias, perfumed gardenias.

He made straight for the bathroom. "The world of a beauty must be adorned with marvels to match her loveliness," he said, and dumped the flowers into the tub.

He came back to the bedroom and stood contemplating her.

"You are so beautiful," he said. "A profile like a cameo, eyes like a cat. You are as beautiful as a Botticelli."

He fell onto one knee and held up his arms as if in worship. "You are as beautiful as my mother, and she was very beautiful indeed."

Then he rose and turned to go. "You will, of course, come to lunch," he said over his shoulder before he left. He closed the door behind him, leaving a trail of petals and bits of flowers behind on the carpet: a rosebud, two purple petunias, and Tamar, standing dumbfounded in the middle of the room.

She gathered the scattered remnants of petals from the carpet, laid them on the table next to the breakfast tray and went into the bathroom. She took off the robe and wondered how to deal with the stemless flowers that smiled up at her and filled the bottom two inches of the tub. She turned on the water and stepped into the shower. The flowers crunched beneath her feet. She stood on the floral carpet beneath the stream from the showerhead, savoring the bite of hot water, steam and perfume from the flowers filling her nostrils. She thought about the mad, handsome Italian who had invaded the bathroom, then left, and she began to sing.

It wasn't until later, after she was fully dressed and had combed her hair, that she wondered about the ghostly image of Chatham on a television station that came from a place she didn't know and told a story in a language she didn't understand.

Chapter Thirteen

Sofia, Bulgaria, August 12, 1990

Irena read about the body found in the outskirts of Sofia in the *Vecherni Novini*, the *Evening News*.

The dead man had no identification, no packages, empty pockets, only a label in his suit from a tailor in Savile Row in London that raised the possibility that the corpse was British.

She had to wait until the next day, Monday, before she could call the British Museum and ask for Chatham. She was told he hadn't arrived yet. She asked when he was expected.

"Last week," the woman from the Department of Near Eastern Antiquities told her. "He seems to be delayed. We've had no word from him."

"It's him," she told Dimitar. "The corpse in the newspaper. I'm sure it's Chatham. How can we claim the insurance without him?"

It was bad enough that the locker at the airport was empty, with no sign of the suitcase or the gold, and now this.

"We wait," Dimitar said, and picked up the paper to read the article himself.

Irena was fuming. They had worked so hard, and this time, nothing went right.

Who expected that stupid Chatham to send two *bortsi* to the hospital? And that Italian, or Swiss, or whatever he was. The arrangement they made in Turkey was for him to rescue

Chatham in the park after the robbery and pour him on the plane so he could contact Lloyd's.

Not this. You can't trust anyone anymore.

She rubbed her arm with irritation. "We should go to the police and identify him."

"We can't do that. Our identity cards are suspect. God knows what they will think. That we are spies, maybe? We could get shot."

"I'll go. I'll smile and they won't look too closely at my identity card." She paused a moment to think. "Wait. I have an old British passport somewhere. I'll go as a concerned friend."

"The passport's too old. It's expired."

"Fix it. I'll go this afternoon."

After lunch, armed with a well-worn but current British passport, she went to the police and told them that she was concerned about her traveling companion, a man who had gone missing. She waited in the reception hall of the station for two hours seated on a hard wooden bench, and then they brought her to the morgue.

"It's not a pleasant sight," the man said. "The wild dogs..."

He brought her to a well-scrubbed room of tile and stainless steel that smelled of alcohol and rot. The man went through a door and reappeared behind a glass at the far end of the room and beckoned to her.

The room beyond the glass had a steel gurney in the center holding a body covered with a sheet. The man pulled back the sheet.

The face was recognizable but the dogs had done their work on his arms and upper body.

"It's Chatham," she said, and fainted. When she came to, she asked the man if he found the suitcase that Chatham carried.

"There was nothing found with him," the policeman told her. "Not so much as a handkerchief."

"We have to give a report," he said. He took the information from her passport and turned to her to ask a question.

"I think I'm going to faint again," she said, holding her head. "I must lie down."

"You had a great shock," he said.

"Can we finish the report tomorrow?"

He offered to drive her to the British Embassy. She asked him to drive her to her hotel instead, repeated that she needed to lie down. She promised to return the next day so that he could complete the report.

He said he understood and drove her to the new hotel, the Sheraton at Sveta Nedelya Square where she told him she was staying. She thanked him at the curb and assured him she would be all right by the next day. She went through the lobby, took the elevator to the eighth floor, then the stairs back down to the lobby. She left the hotel by the Largo Street entrance and crossed the street to the Archaeological Museum. She stayed there for an hour, looking at the exhibits, and then took a taxi back to the apartment on Rakovsky.

Chapter Fourteen

Basel, Switzerland, August 12, 1990

The table in the dining room was set for three, but only Tamar and Gilberto were there, waiting for lunch.

When her taxi arrived at Gilberto's that morning, she saw a heavy-set man who seemed to be sneering, hunched at the side entrance to the basement. When he saw Tamar, he ducked back inside. Probably just a friend of Fabiana's, Gilberto said when she told him about it.

"I can make you my agent in the United States, set you up in business," Gilberto was saying. His voice was as seductive as cream. If she weren't careful, she would slide into agreement with him.

"I'm an archaeologist, not an antiquities dealer," Tamar said.

"You can't make a decent living at it. Not enough to live well." He leaned forward and touched her arm. "I can make you rich."

She clutched the edge of the table. "I couldn't. It's unethical."

"To be rich?"

"To deal in antiquities."

"Once I thought the same, when I studied archaeology—in Florence, in Rome at the Pontifical Institute, at the Sorbonne." He waved his glass with the Bloody Mary in her direction as if he were offering a toast and almost spilled some on the carpet. "Elegance, my dear, elegance is what you need, and enough money to live elegantly."

His hands moved eloquently, enticingly as he spoke. "If the Elgin Marbles were not in the British Museum, where would they be today? Blown up in a Turkish ammunition depot?" Even his hair was sensuous, black and lush, with the silver accent at the temples. "If Napoleon left the Rosetta stone in a little town in the Egyptian delta, what would we know of ancient Egypt?"

"That's sophistry, intellectual imperialism."

"Besides," he said with a lift of his head as if settling the argument, "the Elgin Marbles were bought and paid for from the Ottoman Empire, the legitimate government of the time."

Tamar found herself getting angry. "That was a deliberate political ploy on the part of the Turkish government. If you sell the past, you lose it, lose the meaning of it, lose the human heritage. It's immoral."

"Immoral? Unethical? How so? Moral choice requires an ability to embrace ambiguity." He took a sip of the Bloody Mary and put the glass on the table next to the coaster. "I just do the same as the ancient Greeks and Italians. In ancient times Etruscans bought and sold objects of art, traded them, brought Greek pottery to grace a wealthy Etruscan's afterlife." He moved his glass to the coaster and traced his finger along the ring the glass had left. "Now we find Greek pottery in Etruscan tombs. The pottery is part of my heritage and I do with it as I think best."

"So you do well by doing good?"

"Yes, I do good. You think dealing in antiquities is evil?" he asked.

"If it's not evil, it leads to evil."

"We can only understand evil by looking within ourselves. We all keep a bit of it there. In evil, everyone is an accomplice, everyone is a victim. We excuse ourselves, and point the finger the other way. The blame is always on them, them, them."

The doorbell sounded. Tamar heard Fabiana grumble as she shuffled along the back hall from the kitchen to answer the door. Voices echoed from the foyer, and Enzio appeared at the entrance to the dining room. He carried a small, battered gym bag in his right hand.

"You have something for me?" Gilberto asked.

Enzio raised the bag and nodded.

"Good, we'll take care of it after lunch."

This time, the lunch began with steak tartar spiked with scotch and went on endlessly, with beefsteak and side dishes, tomato salad, and ice cream drizzled with maraschino for dessert.

When they finished, Gilberto turned to Tamar. "Come along, my dear. We go downstairs. You can learn about the business, see how evil it really is."

He led the way down a narrow curved stairway, and Tamar followed, groggy from the Bloody Mary and the two glasses of wine at lunch. They entered a small room with a brick floor burnished to a luster. In the center, four black leather sling chairs with chromium legs faced a chrome and glass coffee table. Funerary stelae of men in the prime of life, their heads bowed in grief, of desolate Greek youths being led into eternity by long-nosed dogs, of coifed matrons draped on lounges and gazing into mirrors, lined the room.

An alcove on the far wall held a wine cellar, stacked floor to ceiling on all three walls with wine bottles that sat in their pigeonholes like ancient manuscripts in a columbarium.

"We go into the workroom," Gilberto said and led the way through a door in the far wall to a room with two waist-high workbenches covered with carpeting. Shelves crammed with jars and cups filled with tubes and brushes lined the walls.

Gilberto took the bag from Enzio and spilled the contents onto a worktable. Painted pottery sherds tumbled onto the table and Gilberto began to match broken bits of pottery to each other as if he were working a jigsaw puzzle.

"A black on red." He picked up a piece of curved rim and a handle and held them about three inches apart, narrowing his eyes as if envisioning the whole vessel. "A jug. An *oinichoe*."

"I found it in an Etruscan cemetery, near Civita Castellana," Enzio said.

Tamar edged closer to the workbench, craning her neck to see around Gilberto's left arm. "They're all fresh breaks. You broke this yourself?" she asked Enzio.

"Easier to take out of Italy. I drove up over the Alps, through San Bernardino Pass. The border there is more user-friendly."

Gilberto dropped a sherd on a small wooden side table. It made a dull clunk. He tried another. The same deadened sound.

He turned to Tamar and handed her a sherd. "What can you tell me about this *oinichoe*?"

"From the sound when you bounced it on the table, I'd say it was fired at a low temperature."

Gilberto nodded and smiled, encouraging her to go on.

"And the color of the cross section—gray with red inclusions—I'd say that confirms a low firing temperature, with older pottery grout."

"And?" Gilberto tilted his head at her. "Go on. Why would someone make pottery like that?"

"To get around thermoluminescence."

"How would that work?"

"It's a very simple principle. All clay contains some radioactive impurities. They emit alpha, beta, and gamma rays, causing ionization that is trapped inside the clay and increases at a steady rate over time. When the clay is fired above a certain temperature, the charge is released in the form of light. The firing is the zero point. After the clay is fired the charge begins to accumulate again. The longer the time period, the greater the charge. The greater the charge, the more light is emitted, and the more time since the pot was fired."

"What does that have to do with what you noticed, the gray core and the pottery grout?"

"The gray core and the dull thud when the sherd was dropped on the table mean that the pot was fired at a low temperature, probably below the point at which ionization would be cleaned out."

"And the red pottery grout?"

"Most clay is too slippery to work and needs rough inclusions—temper, or grout—so that it holds its shape. The potter used ground-up bits of ancient pots as temper. Those are the red bits. The pot was fired at a temperature low enough not to reset the ionization, so thermoluminescence would give a false, ancient date because of the red grout."

"Now look at this," Gilberto said. He took down a bottle from a shelf and a wad of cotton. "Simple nail polish remover," he said, wetting the wad of cotton and rubbing it over the surface of one of the sherds. The paint smudged. "It is impossible to imitate the process the Greeks used to paint pottery. If this were genuine, it would not smudge. Besides," he said, putting two of the sherds together to form a part of the figure of a man with a spear, "this *oinichoe* is a copy of one published in Beasely."

"Beasely?" Tamar said.

"The corpus of classical Greek pottery." Gilberto shook his head. "Enzio, Enzio. Not even a good imitation." He gave another nod and a mournful glance. "My oldest friend. How could you do this to me?"

His jaw worked in anger. He held the gym bag open against the edge of the table, swept the pottery sherds into the bag and turned to go. He shoved the bag at Enzio.

"Don't speak to me. The last time you did this, one of my runners landed in jail, and I was almost arrested myself," he said and stomped out and up the stairs.

Tamar looked after him.

"You knew it was fake," she said to Enzio.

"So did you. You did that very well," Enzio said. "How did you figure it out?"

"I have the fine, analytical mind of an archaeologist."

"That would account for your conjectures about the pottery. And your lecture about scientific dating?"

"Hell, I teach it."

"That explains it."

"You listen well. When I give this lecture in my Intro class, the students' eyes glaze over."

"I was fascinated by your ability to infer so much from the color and sound of a piece of pottery."

"What was that about? Why bring a fake *oinichoe* to Gilberto?"

"It's just an old joke we have between us, that's all."

"You know Gilberto well?"

"Of course I know Gilberto. I've known him a long time. I knew him when his name was still Sergio Benetti. We were children together, playing in the slums of Naples. He spent a lot of time around the museum, sometimes begging for pennies on the steps outside, sometimes in the halls drinking in the sight of statues and vases, memorizing them."

"That's what inspired him to go to the university?"

"What university? One day he stole a wallet from one of the tourists in the museum, almost got caught. He grabbed the money and ran to the railroad station, hopped on the first train. It was going to Bologna."

"He studied in Bologna?"

"You could say that. The museum there uses old men as guards. They fall asleep and the museum cases aren't always locked. He stole a *kylix*—one of those graceful drinking cups with a high base and handles on either side that the Greeks used for wine. Red on black with a fine drawing of a drinking scene on the tondo. He hid it under his coat. He came back to Naples and told me how easy it was. He sold the *kylix* to someone and said he was going back to Bologna, had an order for a *lykethos*. I didn't see him again until he turned up here in Basel as Viscount Gilberto Dela Barcolo."

"He lies a lot?"

"He doesn't think of it as lying. He thinks of it as embellishing, just fills in the blanks with his imagination," he said.

But still, it bothered her. "Neither of you can be trusted."

"Don't misunderstand me. I like Gilberto very much. He's a man with a wealth of misinformation at his fingertips. It's gratifying to find someone who is more deceptive than I am. Besides, he's my oldest friend."

Enzio opened the door to the other room and went to the wine alcove. He reached for a bottle of wine and inspected the label. "Ah, Blanc de Blanc, Rothschild 1983. That will do. Let's go upstairs."

Upstairs, he handed the bottle to Gilberto. "A peace offering."

"Now he tries to bribe me with my own wine," said Gilberto, looking at the label. "Enzio, Enzio, you are incorrigible. What am I going to do with you?" He put the bottle on the table and reached into a drawer for a corkscrew. "This calls for a special observance." He opened the wine with a resounding pop and strode to the door. "Fabiana," he shouted.

She appeared through the dining room, a dishcloth in one hand, untying an apron with the other.

"Some ice and a *torte di inglese*."

She stood in the door of the dining room, glaring at Gilberto, the apron hanging loose from the straps around her neck. "*Per favore?*" she said.

"*Scusi*." Gilberto gave a slight bow. "*Per favore*."

"No pablum," she answered.

"No problem?" Enzio said.

"That's what I said. No pablum."

Fabiana flounced out to the kitchen and reappeared in a few minutes without the apron, carrying a tray with a bucket of ice, plates, a cake, and four champagne flutes.

"*Grazie*," she said, as if she were giving an order.

Gilberto bowed again and reached for the tray. "*Grazie*," he said and rested the tray on the coffee table, gently laid the bottle of wine in the ice bucket, and began to twirl it while Fabiana seated herself in a chair in front of the fireplace. Gilberto carefully poured out four glasses and handed them around.

When they finished the wine and the cake, Tamar left, deciding that a walk back to the Euler would clear her head. As she stood on the steps outside of Gilberto's, she noticed a plump gray-haired man leaving by the cellar door. He seemed to be sneering. He gave Tamar a steely-eyed glance as he strode off.

◇◇◇

Back at the Euler, dizzy and headachy from too much wine and wondering about Enzio and his performance at Gilberto's, Tamar fell on the bed and slept for the rest of the afternoon. In her dreams, she saw her grandmother's stern face and heard her angry voice, "Too young, too young. You should have gone with them," and ached for her lost parents and her brothers.

When she awakened, she still had a slight headache. The dream haunted her, and the memory of the terrible day that she heard about the accident that killed her parents and brothers.

The dream was about Alex too, she thought. I should have been with them, she told herself, plagued by a vague notion that somehow her presence would have changed things.

She had dinner in her room and then went downstairs to the bar to buy a bottle of water.

Enzio sat at one of the tables. He waved her over and she joined him. She was still bothered by his attempt to fob off the fake *oinichoe* on Gilberto, but she had become used to the talks they had since the first night she arrived in Basel.

The waiter brought a sherry and a bottle of Evian water for her and a Campari for Enzio, just as he had every evening.

She leaned back in her chair and asked, "Did you also have another name, before you became Enzio?"

"As a matter of fact, I did. My name was Aldo. So, of course, I changed it. Every Tom, Dick, and Harry is named Aldo."

Beads of moisture had formed on the side of the water bottle. Tamar trailed her finger along it.

"Your English is very good," she said.

"I spent two years in Brooklyn. It's kind of a rite of passage. Almost every Italian spends two years in Brooklyn, even Mussolini. He spent two years there when he was a journalist."

She took the small paper napkin from under her sherry glass and wiped the side of the water bottle. "And Gilberto? Did Gilberto spend two years in Brooklyn?"

"Not Gilberto. Gilberto spent five years in Manhattan."

"How did he manage that?"

"He married a rich American widow. She helped set him up in a shop on Madison Avenue where he sold high end antiquities."

She leaned forward and began to pick at the label on the water bottle. "He's still married to her?"

"They divorced. After her, he came here, married a Swiss woman and got permanent resident status as the husband of a Swiss national. That also lasted five years."

"His relationships have a five year limit?" Tamar asked.

"It's not like that. Each time he falls sincerely in love." He took a sip of Campari and contemplated her. "You're next," he said.

Startled, Tamar sat back in the chair. "What makes you say that?"

"Since he met you, he talks of nothing but the American professor."

She went back to picking at the label. Little bits of paper were falling onto the table. "What does he expect to gain from me?"

"So young and yet so cynical. What about you? Were you ever married?"

Tamar concentrated on the label. "Yes. I was." She brushed the bits of paper from the table into the palm of her hand and stared at them.

"Divorced?" Enzio asked.

She felt tears well in her eyes, blinked them back and continued to look down into the palm of her hand, then shook her head.

"We were doing a survey in the Yucatan," she said. "Alex had found a new Mayan site in the rain forest that no one knew about, hadn't been recorded."

She rubbed the scraps of paper between her palms and dropped them on the table. "The site was overgrown with vegetation, vines, tropical growth. We found some stelae, what looked like the remains of some pyramids and a ball court."

She paused.

"We came on the site by accident, followed a path that had been hacked out in the jungle with a machete."

She took a deep breath, lifted her glass of sherry, looked at it and put it down again.

"He went back by himself to take some record shots, copy some of the glyphs from the stelae. I stayed in town." She had the napkin in her hand and was twisting it at the corners. "He never came back."

She took a sip of the sherry and held her breath for a moment. "They found him in the parking lot of our hotel in the morning, naked, slashed to death with a machete. No one found the site again."

"What about his notes?"

"The notes were gone, the coordinates of the site, the photos were gone."

She ran her fingers up and down the stem of the sherry glass and turned it. Some spilled on the table and she wiped it with the wadded napkin. "I should have been with him."

"You couldn't have saved him," Enzio said.

"But we'd have been together," she said, and once more thought of her grandmother, the way she watched her. Tamar looked like her mother, she knew she did, and her grandmother must have hated her for it. Whenever Tamar walked into her room, her grandmother would fold her arms and tap her foot. Silent. Always silent, she would glare at Tamar as if to ask why Tamar was still alive while the others were all dead.

Tamar took a sip of the sherry while Enzio looked at her. "I was afraid," she said, almost in a whisper.

"Did they ever find whoever killed your husband?" he asked.

She shook her head. "Never. Parts of the stelae showed up a year later in museums."

All the frustration and anger and self-guilt of the past three years welled up in her.

"They're all in on it," she said with a sweeping gesture. The bottle of water tipped over and began to roll off the table. "From the *esteleros* in the Yucatan to the *tombaroli* who rob tombs in Tuscany, to the runners and dealers and the collectors. Gilberto included. Even the museums."

Enzio retrieved the bottle of water from the floor and handed it to her.

"And what about you?" she asked. "What was that trick you pulled today with the *oinichoe*? Are you a *tombaroli* or are you a con man?"

After a moment of silence, he said, "You're not here to buy something for a museum. You're here to get some kind of redemption."

She considered that for a while and then thought maybe what he said was true.

Chapter Fifteen

London Times, August 14, 1990

BRITISH ARCHAEOLOGIST
KILLED IN BULGARIA

SOFIA, BULGARIA— British archaeologist Andrew Chatham, Assistant Keeper of Near Eastern Archaeology at the British Museum and lecturer at Izmir University, was found murdered here three days ago.

Chatham's corpse was discovered fully clothed, face down outside an abandoned warehouse in the outskirts of Sofia. Preliminary autopsy reports indicate that the cause of death was a blunt head trauma. The body had been stripped of all identification.

Police are investigating robbery as a possible motive, but are asking the public's help in identifying any potential suspects.

Chatham is best known as one of the principal excavators of Tepe Hazarfen, where he unearthed some noteworthy Chalcolithic tombs, remarkable for their well-preserved pottery and tomb furnishings. A spokesman at the British Museum said that more recently he was working in eastern Bulgaria (ancient Thrace), where he recovered a singular hoard of Thracian gold that he was transporting to the museum. The gold has not been found.

A woman who claimed to be his traveling companion, Irene Conway, who has disappeared, tentatively identified Chatham's body. His wife, Emma, who has accompanied his body to their home in Turkey for burial, has since confirmed Chatham's identity.

Inquiries at the address on Rakofsky Street that was Chatham's last known address revealed an empty apartment that had been rented for the past month to a Russian national who went by the name of Dimitri Karamazov, the name of a principal character in the well-known *Brothers Karamazov*, by Dostoyevsky.

Chapter Sixteen

Basel, Switzerland, August 15, 1990

They arrived in Basel from Germany in the late morning, registered at the Drei Konig Hotel as Mr. and Mrs. Demitrius Konstantinopoulis, and handed the desk clerk Greek passports.

They had come to find the gold. They had already checked out antiquities dealers in Berlin, posing as shipping magnates, collectors of ancient gold jewelry. When they asked specifically for Thracian gold, no one had any to offer. Now they were ready to try for the gold in Basel, ready to start with the foremost antiquities dealer in Switzerland.

"Early this afternoon," Demitrius said after they had settled in, "we start with Gilberto Dela Barcolo."

Irena still fumed about Chatham's betrayal. "He lied about the insurance," she said again. "And then, to get himself killed." She looked into the mirror above the desk and smoothed her hair, tucked a strand behind her left ear, and turned her head to check the effect. "We could be blamed. We could get into trouble. We didn't arrange for that."

"Neither did Chatham," Demitrius told her. "There's someone else betraying us, and they will pay the price."

Tamar stood in the foyer at Gilberto's house looking down at the mosaic on the floor. "That's what I mean," she said. "Something for the entrance of the museum. A mosaic, perhaps."

Gilberto nodded and his hands blocked out an expansive area. "A fresco." He smiled and moved his hands as though outlining a decoration in front of him. "My runner has arranged to purchase a fresco from a Roman villa near Pompeii that was buried in the eruption. The owner himself dug it out."

"I was thinking more of a mosaic floor."

"That also, but it needs restoration. Come, I'll show you."

He led her into the salon and went into the adjacent alcove, opened the drawer of a marquetry chest and brought out a photograph. "This is the fresco. From the triclinium, the dining room."

"And the mosaic floor?"

"We are presently restoring in my warehouse."

She looked at the photograph for a moment, then returned it. "You have a picture of the mosaic?"

"Not yet."

"Both are from Pompeii?"

"Not Pompeii. Another village in the shadow of Vesuvius, buried in the same eruption," he told her.

Maybe it really was from Italy, maybe she should look elsewhere for the mosaic.

"I would like to see it," she said.

"The ash and tuff from the eruption must be removed carefully. Right now it's not in condition to be seen. Another few days, perhaps."

He walked back to the chest and put the photograph away. "Meanwhile, I have a gift for you," he said. "A beautiful gift for a beautiful woman."

He opened another drawer and held out a spiral bracelet of ancient gold with a horse's head and bit at one end and a coiled tail at the other.

"It's Thracian," he said. "You know of the Thracians, of course, who Herodotus called the wild people of the north." He dangled the bracelet lovingly from his index and middle finger. "Thrace, the land where the Boreal Winds blow, the land of Dionysus, the land of the Hellespont and even the land of Byzantium, long before Constantine built his marvels and monuments there to rule his empire."

The harsh ring of the doorbell interrupted him.

He waved his hand and moved closer. "Fabiana will answer it. I am expecting visitors from Greece."

He reached for Tamar's hand and wound the bracelet around her arm.

"I can't accept it," Tamar said.

He patted her hand and smiled. "No strings attached."

"It's an artifact. As an archaeologist...."

The visitor was Enzio, not the Greeks whom Gilberto expected.

Enzio leaned against the doorjamb and smiled at Tamar. "Take the bracelet," he said. "It's all right."

She shook her head.

"Trust me," Enzio said.

Gilberto looked from Enzio to Tamar and back again. "Can she trust you, Enzio? Can either of us trust you?"

She felt the weight of it. It was real gold. "It's too valuable," she said. Besides, what did he expect in return?

The doorbell sounded again, with the bracelet still on her wrist.

"Ah, my Greek visitors, at last," Gilberto said.

Demitrius entered the room with a rush, carrying a battered cardboard suitcase. He laid it on the table in front of Gilberto, then stood back dramatically waiting for a comment. Instead, Gilberto made introductions all around.

Demitrius stared at the bracelet on Tamar's wrist, took her hand, and bent low to kiss it. He straightened up and nodded at Irena, still grasping Tamar's hand, turning it slightly so that the bracelet glinted in the light.

After a few moments, he dropped her hand and gestured toward the battered suitcase.

"I give you the privilege of opening it," he said to Gilberto.

"You brought me something?"

"Something marvelous."

Gilberto reached for the suitcase, unsnapped the lock, opened it, and lifted out a gold pendant of Aphrodite. He held it to the light, said "*Perbacco*," put it on the table and took out another piece.

"*Belle cose*, beautiful things," he said, almost in a whisper. "It's the Bactrian hoard."

He lifted a golden crown, balanced it on the open palm of his left hand and traced along the edge with a finger of his right hand. "Beautiful. How did you find it?"

"That's only part of what I have." Demitrius looked at the others as if he expected appreciative comments and, again, his gaze stopped at the bracelet on Tamar's wrist.

"The rest I have in a vault," Demitrius said more slowly.

Gilberto lifted a coin. "A gold drachma with the head of Alexander." He reached into the drawer of the table, took out a jeweler's loupe and a knife, picked up the Aphrodite again, and scraped at it with the knife. "Solid gold," he said. He turned to Demitrius. "All this was found together?"

"I have a dagger studded with jewels, twenty thousand coins, all from the same collection," he said, still looking at Tamar's arm. "Seven tombs in northern Afghanistan excavated in the seventies by a Soviet archaeologist. All of it disappeared when they invaded Afghanistan."

"And you found it?"

Demitrius inhaled deeply, looked around the room, and concentrated again on the bracelet on Tamar's arm. Irena followed his gaze and moved toward Tamar. She seemed ready to reach for the bracelet.

Tamar didn't notice. She was watching Enzio and saw him move to the suitcase and peer inside, saw him flick his finger, quick as a lizard's tongue, and pocket a coin.

Was she imagining things? No one else seemed to see it.

Irena grasped Tamar's hand and turned Tamar's wrist this way and that as she examined the bracelet, and finally said, "An unusual piece." She turned Tamar's hand palm up and Tamar began to pull away.

"Lovely. Where did you get it?" Irena asked when she finally released Tamar's hand.

"A gift from a friend," Enzio said.

Tamar hid her arm behind her back and moved away from Irena. I shouldn't be wearing the bracelet, Tamar thought. I should have refused it. But it was Demitrius who stared at Tamar, his lip curled in controlled anger in the silence that followed.

Enzio watched from across the room. He sat in the chair near the fireplace, unbuttoned and rebuttoned his jacket, brushed an imaginary piece of lint from his lapel, and rested his elbow on the arm of the chair.

He crossed his leg over his knee. "That *oinichoe* I brought you," he said to Gilberto. "It came from Mr. Konstantinopoulis."

Demitrius glanced toward the corner of the room. He seemed surprised. "I brought no *oinichoe*."

"You're sure?" Gilberto asked Enzio.

"It passed through the hands of several other parties, but ultimately it came from Mr. K."

"I thought the *oinichoe* came from Italy," Gilberto said.

"And so it did," Demitrius said. "I remember now."

It seemed clear that he didn't remember anything about an *oinichoe*, and he wasn't sure of what they were talking about, but he went on talking, with a depreciating shrug. "I only do the same as the ancient Greeks and Italians. They bought and sold objects of art from Greece, traded them, bought them to grace Etruscan tombs. It's part of my heritage."

"Of course it is," Gilberto said.

"Part of the glory of my heritage," said Demitrius.

"And the Bactrian hoard? Is that also part of your heritage?" Enzio asked.

Demitrius nodded. "The same. After all, Alexander was Greek. You are interested in the gold?"

Gilberto fixed Demitrius with a penetrating look. "The Bactrian hoard came from Greece?"

Demitrius looked at Gilberto as if to challenge him. "Not all Greeks lived in Greece," he said. "Long, long ago, my ancestors

came down from somewhere in the north until they reached
the sea, and with a cry of '*Thalassa, thalassa,*' they changed the
history of the world. Like Vikings of the ancient world, they
spread, first as Myceneans, to the islands, to Crete, to Santorini,
to Troy." He paused, took a breath, and leaned forward. "As
the Sea Peoples, they spread to the Levantine coast, to ancient
Egypt, around the coasts of north Africa. They lived wherever
Ulysses journeyed, in Italy off the Amalfi coast and as far north
as Cumae."

"And carried with them pottery like the red on black
oinichoe?"

"As Greeks they journeyed to Ionia and the Aegean coast of
Turkey, the shores of the Black Sea, to Sicily, to Sardinia, and up
the boot of Italy. Naples was a Greek city, *Nea Polis*. And they
left their pottery to astonish and delight us. You are interested
in the gold?"

Gilberto shook his head. "At the moment...."

"I don't want to sell it," Demitrius said.

"What then?"

"I want to lend it to a museum for an exhibit."

"And you want me to help." Gilbert smiled. "So that it's
authenticated and you get more money for it when you sell it."
He shook his head. "I don't know anyone at the museum."

"The *Antikenmuseum?*"

"Don't know the right people."

Demitrius wiped his hands together in a dismissing gesture,
closed the suitcase, and snapped the lock shut.

"Then we leave." He turned to Tamar. "I can drive you back
to your hotel?"

Enzio stepped in front of her and answered for her. "She has
an appointment."

"I can drive you to your appointment."

"Too far out of your way," Enzio said.

"Where do you stay?" Demitrius asked her.

"Here in Basel," Enzio answered again. "With friends."

◇◇◇

They all left Gilberto's at the same time. Outside, the breeze ruffled Enzio's hair. He and Tamar stood in front of the house as they watched Demitrius and Irena walk toward a dark Mercedes at the far end of the street.

"What was that about?" Tamar asked.

"What?"

"The conversation with Gilberto." She continued to look down the street toward the dark Mercedes. "That's strange. The license plate is Cyrillic, not Greek. You think they could be Russian?"

"I'm not sure. The license is Bulgarian. Car is registered to a Dimitar Konstantinov."

"How do you know that?"

"Konstantinov is a gifted art forger. Lately he's been concentrating on antiquities because that's where the money is."

"He gets away with it?"

"Hasn't been caught yet."

"You know all this for a fact?"

"His time is coming. Now we have their picture."

"Who are 'we'?"

Tamar watched the Mercedes, still idling at the corner. "What is Demitrius waiting for?"

"For you," Enzio said. "Let's walk into town. I'll treat you to an espresso."

"What's the occasion?"

"I have to go away for a few days."

"Back to Italy?"

"France." He waved his hand in the general direction of the river, toward France. "Lyon."

"Lyon?"

"I have to…." He hesitated, contemplated the sky, the clouds gathering above the trees. He examined the street full of cars parked trunk to nose against the curb. The dark Mercedes was gone now. "I have to visit my mother."

"I thought you came from Naples."

"My mother lives in Lyon."

"Why Lyon?"

"She likes the food. Best in France." He put his hands in his pockets and gazed at Tamar. "You'll be careful when I'm gone?"

"I'll look both ways before I cross the street."

"You do that. The Greek couple, Demitrius Konstaninopoulis and his wife, they're not what they seem. And they could be dangerous. Be careful. They may kill if they find out you're on to them."

"You're not what you seem either," Tamar said. "I saw you pocket the coin."

Chapter Seventeen

Basel, Switzerland, August 15, 1990

All the way back to the Euler, Tamar checked the road behind her taxi and watched for signs that Konstantinopoulis had followed her, even suspicious of the cars in side streets that waited for traffic to pass before they made a turn. Once she spotted a dark blue Mercedes through the rear window and began to panic until she noticed the Swiss plates. Still, she breathed easier when the Mercedes pulled to the curb and parked before they reached the turn at Aeschenplatz.

She arrived at the hotel without incident and went straight to her room. I'm just foolish, she thought. Enzio must be wrong. No one is after me.

She lifted her arm to brush a tuft of stray hair and realized she was still wearing the bracelet. She wrenched it off her wrist as if it were contaminated, wrapped it in a tissue from the bathroom and hid it in the dresser drawer under her underwear, determined to give it back next time she saw Gilberto.

She sat in the chair by the window, thinking about the mosaic, pondering what she must do to find it. Gilberto, charming as he was, was a dead end.

I'm not made for this, she thought. I dig holes in the ground; I do research, analyze tools and bits of ceramics in laboratories and examine old collections in museums.

This is also research, she told herself, and decided to try a more direct approach, starting with the museum. She crossed over to the telephone and found the listing for *Antikenmuseum* in the hotel handbook, called the Antiquities Museum and asked for the head curator.

After a few clicks, a woman's voice answered. "*Hochstadtler hier.*"

Tamar hesitated, unsure of what to say next. "This is Doctor Saticoy," she began.

"The American professor," Hochstadtler said.

"You know who I am?"

"We are a tight little community. I even know what you have for lunch. Gossip keeps us busy, keeps us out of trouble."

Tamar made an appointment for later that afternoon and left the Euler. With time to kill, she took a leisurely stroll to St. AlbanGraben, stopping along the way at a coffee bar for filtered coffee and a gelato. She sat at a table outside, absentmindedly watching housewives marching home laden with packages and children running, laughing as they left school playgrounds. Sometimes a man passed, once a man in a polo shirt with a leather bag hanging from his wrist, another time a man wearing a dark suit and carrying a briefcase.

She looked at her watch and saw that she still had a couple of hours to spare. She had heard about the *Kunstmuseum*, about how the city voted to buy two Picassos in a referendum, and how Picasso, touched by a city's appreciation of art, donated four more.

She made her way to the *Kunstmuseum* at the end of the street, walked around Rodin's *Les Bourgeois de Calais* that stood at the entrance, smiled at the portly, self-important men of Calais, and went inside. She paid the entrance fee and bought a catalogue at the desk.

The Picassos were on the second floor. On the first floor, she lingered at the Holbeins, examining paintings of Erasmus and the good burghers of Basel, then went upstairs to walk amid Picassos, Braques, Klees with lollipop faces, until it was time to leave for the *Antikenmuseum*.

She found the staff entrance of the Antiquities Museum on the side of the building—a small door next to the loading dock—went inside and told the guard at the desk that she had an appointment with Dr. Hochstadtler. He folded his newspaper and asked her to wait, pointing to a bench near the door, picked up a telephone and murmured something into the mouthpiece.

"A minute," he said to Tamar and went back to his newspaper.

Before the minute had passed, Dr. Hochstadtler, a small woman with ash blond hair and dimpled cheeks, came clicking down the hall.

She smiled at Tamar and shook her hand vigorously. "Always good to meet a colleague."

She led the way to her office along a corridor crammed with crates and painted backdrops for displays. "Please excuse the mess," she said. "We're getting ready for a new exhibit. Opens Tuesday."

They reached her office and she gestured toward the seat facing the desk. "I have only a few minutes."

"Dr. Hochstadtler…" Tamar hesitated, not sure of how to begin.

"Maria, please."

"Has anyone offered you a mosaic floor from a Roman villa?" Tamar asked.

"You asked Gilberto? I heard he recently acquired one."

"That one is from a villa near Pompeii. I'm looking for one from Turkey."

"Turkey?"

"It was stolen from my site."

The curator shook her head and sighed. "There's a lot of that lately. It's getting worse." She crossed her arms. "We won't deal with things like that. We always check for provenance." She looked over at Tamar. "I can keep an eye out. You have pictures?"

"The mosaic disappeared overnight, before we had time to photograph it."

Maria pondered for a moment, fingering her chin with her thumb. "Come to dinner tonight. Leandro Aristides will be there. He might know. He's from Istanbul, a specialist in Turkish antiquities. He keeps his ear to the ground, has radar that picks up everything."

Tamar returned to the Euler and found a message from Gilberto. She called and he asked if she could come for lunch, that he had something interesting to show her. "Not tomorrow," he said. "I have to be elsewhere. Friday. Make it Friday. Tell Enzio to come along too, if you see him."

She told him that Enzio was in Lyon, visiting his mother.

"His mother is dead," Gilberto said. "Died a long time ago. They were close. When she died, he changed his name to Enzio, her maiden name." He paused. "Lyon, you say?"

"Is that significant?"

"He goes there lately. Before that, he went to Paris." He paused again. "Never mind. I think I know. Friday then, for lunch."

The evening at Hochstadtler's began with Tamar proffering a bouquet of five roses and, again, vigorous handshakes all around—to Maria Hochstadtler and her husband, to their two daughters, chestnut-haired and solemn like their father, dimpled like their mother.

They all look like Holbeins, she thought. Everyone in Basel looks like a Holbein to me, and she wondered if she had spent too much time wandering the *Kunstmuseum*.

"Maximillian Hochstadtler," Maria's husband said as he pumped Tamar's arm. "Call me Max."

"Tamar Saticoy. Call me Tamar."

"Ah! The American professor. Friend of Gilberto Dela Barcolo." He smiled. "Gilberto of the red carpet." The last was said with a bit of disdain, as if the red carpet that covered the stairs at the entrance to Gilberto's house were a little too ostentatious, a little indecent, and hinted of worse going on inside.

Tamar looked around the room, at the cherry wood trim around doors and windows, at the cream colored walls. The taupe sofa and staid brown leather chairs gathered decently around a mahogany coffee table, the lawyer's bookcase with cloth books neatly lined up at the lip of the shelves, the slightly faded oriental rug all contrasted with the sybaritic splendor of Gilberto's house.

Max kept talking without stop. He was a chemist who worked for one of the pharmaceutical houses in Basel, he told Tamar. He apologized for polluting the Rhine and asked how she liked the city, how she liked the museums, if she had visited the *tiergarten*, the zoological garden.

"I was at the *Kunstmuseum* this afternoon," she said.

"Ah, then you met my ancestors."

He disappeared with a smile into another room and came back carrying a postcard.

"The family Hochstadtler," he said and handed her the card with a flourish.

It was a photograph of a painting from the museum, a Holbein. No wonder they look like Holbeins, Tamar thought, scanning their faces. All of Basel is full of living, four-hundred-year-old Holbeins.

◇◇◇

"Leandro was an antiquities dealer. He's from Istanbul originally," Maria was telling Tamar in the kitchen as she found a vase for the roses while her daughters filled bowls of ox-tail soup. "He sold a Byzantine collection to Dumbarton Oakes for over two million dollars and retired. Now he's working for his own pleasure, but he still knows what's going on in the market. Not much gets past him."

The kitchen was not like the other rooms Tamar had seen. It was another world, slick white and stainless steel, with bins that opened and shut and pulled out with the touch of a button.

When the doorbell rang, Maria signaled her daughters to finish ladling the soup and rushed into the foyer. Tamar followed.

Leandro Aristides, balding, mustachioed like a Turk, arrived breathless and smiling and carrying a bottle of wine. He presented his exquisite, elegant wife. The astonishingly beautiful Madame Aristides, with her dark hair, thick and shining and tinged with auburn, and her sad, russet eyes, stood next to him almost motionless, inclining her head slightly through a new round of handshakes. On the middle finger of her right hand, she wore an enormous, luminous pearl as faultless as her face.

Dinner began with the ox-tail soup, followed by Coquille St. Jacques, then veal and morels cooked in a cream sauce.

Tamar sat across the table from Aristides' wife and gazed at the pearl and watched Madame Aristides pushing food around on her plate with her fork. She ate little, just picked at the seafood of the Coquille St. Jacques and moved it to the side of the plate.

"In the beginning," Madame Aristides said to Tamar as she saw Tamar stare at the pearl, "God created a white jewel from his own precious soul."

Aristides looked startled. He seemed to give his wife a warning look of disapproval, and Tamar turned away.

"The dinner is delicious," she said to Maria, and saw Aristides' wife move another scallop to the side. "You're a true gourmet cook."

Maria shrugged and smiled and tilted her head. "Don't be so impressed. The soup was Knorr, the Coquille St. Jacques come from the ready food counter at the Coop. For the rest of the dinner my daughters helped. The menu is typically Swiss, typically Basler."

"And what brings you to Basel?" Aristides asked.

"I'm looking for a mosaic floor from a Roman villa."

Aristides raised his eyebrows in question. "Gilberto has one." He leaned back in his chair and contemplated Tamar. "You know that, don't you?"

Tamar's fork hovered over her plate. Could Aristides be trusted? She looked across at the silent Madame Aristides, who didn't smile, who didn't move her mouth. Her perfect face was expressionless, as if she were afraid that any emotion would leave scars.

It was Maria who broke the silence. "Tamar is looking for one that was stolen from her site."

"What site is that?" he asked.

Tamar put down her fork and played with the napkin on her lap. "Tepe Hazarfen," she said at last.

"Tepe Hazarfen? In Turkey?" Aristides narrowed his eyes and contemplated her. "I know someone who may be able to help you. He'll be coming in to Basel tomorrow. I'll make inquiries."

Maria's daughters cleared the plates and emerged from the kitchen with slices of apples arranged on a board around an enormous wheel of cheese.

"From the mountains," Maria told her guests. "This cheese is found only in Switzerland. Too delicate to export."

They ended the dinner with crisp, tart slices of apple and with cheese spread on segments of Basel's special hard rolls.

Before they left for the evening, Aristides told Tamar to come by his place the day after next. "I'll introduce you to the man I'm expecting." He reached into his pocket and took out a card case. "We are at Engelgasse 7, Apartment 7A," he said and handed a one of the cards to Tamar. "Eleven o'clock."

Tamar crossed her arms across her chest in the chill evening air as she got into the taxi to drive back to the Euler. It had begun to drizzle. By the time she reached the hotel, it was pouring. She ran through the rain into the lobby. Before she went upstairs, she stopped in the bar to buy a bottle of water and looked around for Enzio before she remembered that he had gone to Lyon. She was surprised at how much she missed their nightly chat.

Herr Keller was in the bar, ready to spend a long evening talking. He asked if she were enjoying her stay, how she liked Basel, if she had been to the museums, how she liked the food.

She told him she had gone to the *Kunstmuseum* and the Antiquities Museum, that she just been to dinner where she ate Swiss specialties—veal with morels, and a cheese from the mountains.

"We have other things," he told her. "Specialties of Basel, like our own chocolates, *Basler Ballen*. You must try them. Buy a few boxes for your friends back in America."

She thought of the department secretaries and the dean who arranged for grants for her summer digs, and asked for the best place to buy the chocolates.

He told her about a shop in Klein Basel, across the river, "Where they make the best *Basler Ballen*. They also do the preserves that we serve with breakfast," he told her and he gave Tamar the address.

Upstairs, her room had been readied for the night. Her bed was opened, the drapes were pulled, and a small glass of cassis stood on the nightstand next to the bed.

She listened to the rain, wondering if Aristides or his friend could give her news about the mosaic. She turned on the floor lamp, dropped into the armchair, and reached for the museum catalogue that she had bought that afternoon. She had left the bookmark on the page about the Holbein, but now the bookmark was wedged between the last page of the catalogue and the cover. She looked around the room. Nothing was as she had left it. There must be a different maid, she thought, someone who rearranges everything, and she felt a little annoyed. And then, foolish.

She dropped the catalogue on the bedside table next to the cassis and examined the room more carefully. The door of the armoire that held the television was open; the television was extended to the end of the track and pointed toward the window. Her shoes were on the other side of the closet, the notepad that was usually next to the telephone was on the table under the catalogue. She pulled open a dresser drawer and found her clothes tumbled and in disarray. She opened the top drawer. The gold bracelet that Gilberto had given her was gone.

She reached for the telephone, asked to speak to Herr Keller, and then decided to go downstairs and report the theft personally. She waited impatiently for the elevator, went down to the lobby, found Herr Keller in the bar, and told him about the missing bracelet.

He seemed insulted. "A gold bracelet, you say?" He called the waiter and ordered a sherry for her. "You looked carefully? You may have misplaced it. Perhaps in your purse? Perhaps a pocket?"

She shook her head and asked him to call the police.

He hemmed and hawed and assured her that everyone on the staff at the Euler was honest, and finally agreed to call the police. She sat forward in the chair, tapping her foot, drumming her fingers on the table, waiting for the police to arrive. Finally a sandy-haired man dressed in a black leather trench coat, Herr Fischer, a detective, swept into the bar and sat at the table next to Tamar.

She repeated the story of the missing bracelet for the detective. She told him it was ancient Thracian gold and he raised his eyebrows. He checked her room, examined the dresser and dusted it for fingerprints.

They went back downstairs and sat in the bar, where she drew a hasty sketch of the bracelet on a napkin for him. He assured her he would call her if he found anything.

When they finished, she went back upstairs, still shaken, feeling violated and imprudent. I should have taken more care, she thought. I should have put it in the hotel safe.

By the time she was ready for bed, the rain had turned to hail and she heard the staccato ping of hailstones against the windows. Then came the thunder, rumbling and crashing with occasional flashes of lightning that penetrated the drapes. She began to count the seconds between the lightning and the claps of thunder, waiting for the storm to come closer and then fade away.

The thunder raged all night, like an angry admonition from the sky. She lay awake, listening to the furious storm. The room filled with static electricity, and seemed to be arcing and sparking as her heart began to pound with a sense of foreboding.

Maybe reading something dull would put her to sleep. In the dark, she felt for the museum catalogue and turned on the lamp. It opened to the page about Holbein.

She began to scan the catalogue and fell into a fitful sleep, conscious of the glow of the lamp, never sure if she was awake or asleep as images of abstract paintings and gold bracelets passed through her head, and a dark Mercedes bore down on her while she was running, running to escape. It's Demitrius, she was saying to Alex as the Mercedes chased her down, Demitrius is the danger.

Chapter Eighteen

Lyons, France, August 16, 1990

He arrived in Lyon at the Gare de la Part-Dieu and took a taxi to the apartment hotel on Boulevard des Belges, right across from the Parc de la Tête d'Or.

He opened the apartment door with the key card he had received in the mail yesterday. He dropped his briefcase on the coffee table and went straight to the computer on the desk in the corner. He turned it on and entered his password, then a second password and a code number. He waited. There was a message for him.

"Onze heure." Eleven o'clock.

He deleted the message and turned off the computer. He wandered into the kitchen and found only an opened box with three stale crackers and some crumbs, and decided to go out to dinner.

He headed for the Rhône. He strolled leisurely, with the park on one side and the river on the other, past the rose garden, heavy with the aroma of damask roses, of tea roses, of old eglantines that wafted toward him. He continued on until he found an upscale *bouchon*, a café with a terrace facing the river on one of the quais. He ordered the specialty of the house, veal sausage—*boudin blanc*—and a bottle of local Beaujolais.

Small sailboats slid along the water, music blaring, with shirtless teenaged boys, laughing and tanned, scrambling on the decks. Small motorboats passed with purple-haired women sunning topless, lying on their backs near the bow.

He contemplated the young women in summer dresses who strolled along the plâge in the evening breeze and thought, with a mighty sigh, how little it took to make him truly content.

He sat on the terrace and watched the river until he noticed the waiter hover near him impatiently. He looked around and saw that he was the last customer. He paid the bill, added a substantial tip, and left.

In the morning, he returned to the same *bouchon* for breakfast.

He ordered what he thought of as a typical French breakfast. He put two spoons of sugar into the fine Limoges cup on the table, and with a pitcher in each hand, simultaneously poured strong French coffee and foaming hot milk into it. He reached for a brioche, still warm from the oven and slick with butter, split it, added a dollop of chevre cheese. He slowly scanned *Le Monde* while eating, sipping his *café-au-lait*, looking up now and then to check for loiterers in the street. He noticed a few pedestrians: an occasional jogger; a couple, immersed in each other, leaning together, arms across each other's shoulders.

He took a second brioche, buttered it, and slathered it with apricot preserves. He bit into the brioche and savored the still fresh, tart-sweet taste of the apricots, glistening and golden, took another sip of *café-au-lait* and leaned back to watch the Rhône.

He checked his watch. Nine o'clock. Still two hours to go.

On an impulse, he left the restaurant and hailed a taxi to take him to the chocolatier on the other side of the Rhône and bought a half-kilo box of chocolates to bring back to Tamar. He took another taxi back to the apartment on the Rive Gauche and dropped off the box of chocolates before he headed for the Quai Charles de Gaulle. He wandered through the streets of *La Cité*, built for tourists and shoppers, and onto a piazza, checked his watch again, and then ducked into the passages that led into Interpol.

At ten forty-eight he stood outside the new Interpol headquarters, gazing at the tall wrought iron fence and the reflecting pool that surrounded it like a medieval moat. A twentieth century version of a medieval castle, he thought as he strolled to the gate.

He stopped at the glass booth at the entrance, gave the guard his card and identification number, and stood passively while the guard subjected him to a body search.

He walked into the public area, the click of his footsteps and the buzz and hum of the glass elevators echoing through the soaring vault of the hollow-sounding atrium. He strolled over to the reception desk where a woman sat behind a console, the tip of her head just visible.

When he reached the desk, she looked up at him with a stern-faced stare.

His French wasn't that good, so he spoke to her in English. "I've come to see my mother."

The receptionist rolled her eyes impatiently and gave him an unsympathetic look. "Your identification, sir."

He sighed, remembering that humor is not appreciated here, took out his wallet and passed the card over to her.

She inspected it and said, "Place your thumb in the receptacle, please," while she typed his name into the computer terminal on the console.

He did what she told him and waited until he saw recognition in her eyes and she nodded when confirmation appeared on her screen. She turned and reached for a plastic card from the shelf behind her.

"Your proximity card, sir." She pointed to the corner of the public area separate from the bank of elevators. "Use that elevator over there, sir. Someone will meet you on the fifth floor."

He sauntered to the elevator, pushed the button, waited for the elevator cage to stop at the lobby floor, and stepped inside. There was a metal plate where there would ordinarily be a panel with buttons for floor selection. He put the "prox" card against the metal plate, the elevator door closed, and the number five appeared above the plate.

The door opened on the fifth floor. A man in a security uniform met him and said, "This way, sir. Follow me."

The guard led him to a glass booth one meter square at the end of the corridor, said, "We have retinal identification, sir," and put his hand on his side-arm.

"Instructions are in three languages, sir. Step one: enter your personal identification number. Step two: place your eye against the scanner when you hear the beep. Step three: after scanning, when you hear the beep, proceed through the door to your left."

For a moment he wondered what would happen if something went wrong. The glass door would lock; he knew that. The guard would shoot him; he knew that. But would the glass go flying? Would poison gas fill the booth? He wasn't going to find out.

He went through the procedure as instructed. The door to the secure area opened. He deposited the "prox" card in the lock box next to the door, continued into a windowless corridor, and entered the office at the end of the hall.

Chapter Nineteen

Basel, Switzerland, August 16, 1990

By morning, the storm had calmed to a steady drizzle. Tamar stood at the window, watching a few pedestrians hurry through the rain, then rang for coffee and a roll. She scanned the *Paris Tribune* that was outside her door while she ate, wondering if there was more news on Chatham's murder, and found nothing. She dressed for the rain in jeans and a tee shirt, put on a yellow slicker and tucked her hair into a rain hat and headed for the taxi stand outside the hotel. She gave the driver the address of the shop that Herr Keller had told her about in Klein Basel, leaned back in the seat, and relaxed.

They drove past the red sandstone Gothic towers of the Münster that stood watch over medieval Basel, and across the Rhine on the Wettstein Bridge.

In a small cobbled square in Klein Basel, red geraniums danced in the window boxes of fourteenth-century half-timbered houses. A trace of sun, just beginning to appear, glinted on the cobbles still shining with rain and dappled the quiet water in the basin of a public fountain fed by a stream of water spouting from the mouth of a stylized griffin. The house on the corner carried a small sign, *Konditurei Basler.*

The shop had three or four tight, low-ceilinged rooms with small fireplaces. Jars of preserves and pastries sat neatly arranged on tables and glass cases.

For a moment, Tamar imagined the house as it had once been, a house where ancestors of the Holbein Baslers once lived in cozy rooms, undersized to protect against the cold, with rag rugs on the floor as a form of insulation and furnished with practical, hand-hewn furniture. How different from nineteenth-century patrician houses like Gilberto's that flaunted the owner's healthy pride in his wealth with central heating and spacious, high-ceilinged rooms and walls covered with watered silk.

Tamar bought two quarter-kilo boxes of *Basler Ballen*, and three jars of preserves: strawberry, raspberry, and apricot. She paid, said, "*Merci, viel mals*" to the woman behind the register, looped the handle of the plastic bag around her wrist, and left the shop.

Outside, the rain had stopped; the little square was bright and clear under a blue sky with occasional gossamer clouds. The cobbles of the street were shining, and leaves on trees were greener from the rainfall. On a day like this, with the world newly washed and under a clean sun, it would be wrong to be indoors. She decided to walk back to the hotel.

She meandered toward the river, humming, swinging the bag of chocolates and preserves from her wrist, passing a red sandstone Gothic church, passing the grounds of the old Carthusian monastery. She strolled down a tree-lined promenade along the bank of the Rhine toward the old bridge, the *Mittlere Brücke*, and began crossing the river on the pedestrian walkway, letting others pass her, cars and buses moving in her peripheral vision, their exhaust dimming the perfection of the day.

She paused in the middle of the bridge and leaned over the concrete railing to look down at the river. Some swimmers cavorted in the Rhine, some pattering a few feet doing a breaststroke, some diving like porpoises. Beneath her feet, she could feel the walkway shudder from the rhythm of the traffic that belched fumes as it hummed across the bridge.

She let go of the railing and saw a dark blue Mercedes turn onto the bridge.

The car moved toward her, slowly at first, picking up speed as it came nearer. The license plate had Cyrillic writing and she could just make out Demitrius Konstantinopoulis at the wheel.

Down in the river, a man was laughing, pitching a bright yellow ball toward a knot of swimmers. A bus moved past her in the center of the bridge, belching diesel fumes, shaking the bridge as it rolled by.

The Mercedes came faster, its wheels slightly canted toward the pedestrian walk. She could see Demitrius' face now, expressionless, determined.

He revved the motor. The Mercedes was aimed at her like a bullet.

People walked past. Cars moved along the bridge. Only the Mercedes stood out, bearing down on her, ready to jump the curb, coming at her faster, faster.

Heart pounding, she moved back against the balustrade. She tried to raise her arm to deflect the blow.

She knew it was coming.

No time to get out of the way.

Her hand caught on the railing. She felt the weight of the package on her wrist. She pulled at it, grabbed for it with her hand.

No time, just seconds to go.

She swung the bag above her head, hurled it at the Mercedes, watched the bag arc toward the windshield of the car.

She saw Demitrius flinch and duck his head, saw him wrench the wheel, saw the car jerk forward, saw the red jam spill across the windshield, saw it shatter into a web of a thousand shards.

The Mercedes leapt onto the walkway and kept going, ramming the yellow posts that flew from its path, smashing through the balustrade.

The balustrade crumbled. The car crashed past it and plunged, nose down, into the Rhine.

Chapter Twenty

The Hague, Netherlands, August 15, 1990

He had just come from the crowded, wind-swept beach at Scheveningen. The place was full of screaming children, running and kicking up sand while their mothers, covered with oil, slept under bright beach umbrellas.

He still had an hour to kill before he met the principals here in The Hague to get paid for the deal. In front of the Ridderzaal, they told him, inside the Binnenhof, right in the middle of the government offices.

Weren't they smart?

He strolled idly down Oude Molenstraat, glancing in shop windows, and wondered if he was being followed.

He looked back to check and noticed a man who had stopped about fifteen meters down the street in front of a store window. He looked like a casual shopper. He carried a shopping bag and wore a dark blue windbreaker, one of those American baseball caps in dark blue and a pair of showy American running shoes, white with blue and black decoration.

He had seen the man before. The man had been following him since Berlin. Did they think he wouldn't notice? Did they think he was stupid?

The man looked too familiar. He had seen the man somewhere else. It had been nagging at him since the first time he spotted the man. Then he remembered. The pictures of the three from Hazarfen, that was where he saw him: Chatham, the girl, and this man.

Orman Çelibi, that was his name. Orman.

He walked about ten meters further and stopped again in front of a cutlery shop with knives and scissors in the window. His reflection in the store window was distorted. It made the scar less noticeable.

Behind him, Orman had stopped, too. I'll have to lose him, Firenzano thought.

An enormous Swiss knife a meter and a half high mounted on a mountain of knives turned round and round, round and round in the middle of the window. Blades and scissors and nail files and key rings and screwdrivers splayed in all directions, as if the knife had tentacles.

He felt for the switchblade in his pocket. He preferred it to a Swiss knife. It was lighter, it was quicker, it was more practical.

If all goes well, he decided, from now on I will call the shots instead of being ordered about.

If all goes well.

He paused and crossed himself with a wish. Right there in the middle of the street, right there with Orman watching.

That was stupid.

He looked around, a little shamefaced, to see if Orman saw him. Orman wasn't there. Relieved, he kept on walking.

Someone on the other side of the street wearing running shoes—white, gray and blue—caught his peripheral vision. He halted a moment and recognized Orman, this time with a white polo shirt; Orman still wore the blue pants. He must have taken off the jacket and cap and put them in the shopping bag.

He knew then that he was being followed by at least two of them, maybe three, someone tracking him on this side of the street, maybe one in front, one behind. The three of them would change places and spell each other like relay runners. Did they think he was stupid?

He looked back again to see if he could spot anyone, then stopped at another shop and looked in the window. Antique furniture.

No one stopped behind him. A man walked past him, brushed against him, and kept going. There must be three of them. Someone was in front, waiting for him to pass.

He crossed the street, his eye on Orman, and stayed behind him. Orman walked faster. He kept pace.

At the corner of Papestraat, he bumped into a man with his head thrown back, dangling a herring over his mouth like a sword swallower about to perform.

What is it with these crazy Dutchmen? They cackle and hauwck when they speak and eat raw herring from a kiosk in the middle of the street.

Next time, he would arrange the meeting himself. Italy, maybe the south of France, somewhere where the food was good.

He turned the corner and saw Orman duck into a doorway. He followed.

After no more than a minute, he came out of the doorway alone and started back toward Molenstraat. He wore the baseball cap and the dark blue windbreaker zipped up to the neck.

He still wore his own shoes. The running shoes didn't fit.

Chapter Twenty-One

Basel, Switzerland, August 16, 1990

As spectators gathered around the gaping parapet and looked down into the Rhine, Tamar backed away. At the edge of the crowd, she shed the rain slicker and hat, turned, and crossed the bridge onto Rheinsprung in Gross Basel.

She walked a few blocks to Markplatz, hailed a taxi, and rode back to the Euler. Her hand trembled as she tried to pay the driver. What did he say? Twenty francs, thirty francs?

She gave him three ten-franc notes and ran into the hotel.

In her room she sat at the desk and gazed into space, still shaking.

She stayed in the chair, not moving for the better part of an hour, then cradled her head in her arms on the desk and closed her eyes. And still, Demitrius' shocked face behind the broken windshield, the sight of the car plunging off the bridge, haunted her. She pictured him, trapped in the car—water swirling around him, gasping for breath—and shuddered.

She turned on the television and watched a man and woman speak to each other in some incomprehensible language, watched shapes move around on the television screen until the room was lit only by the blue light reflected from the screen.

After a while, she realized that she was hungry and went downstairs into the bar. She ordered a filtered coffee, a bottle of water, and the kind of grilled cheese sandwich they made at the bar that they called toast. She sat back and closed her eyes, waiting for the waiter to bring her order.

She opened her eyes when she heard the waiter approach with the sandwich and coffee, and saw Enzio come into the bar, carrying a small package and smiling.

"I brought you something from Lyon," he said and sat next to her.

He put the package in front of her on the table. "For you."

"Can I open it?"

He laughed and nodded.

She removed the wrapper. "Chocolates?"

"What did you think I would bring?"

She knew she should thank him, but all she could think of was the package of *Basler Ballen* and the shattered windshield after she had hurled it.

She took a sip of coffee. It burned her mouth. Her hand began to shake, and she gripped the handle of the cup so hard that it snapped. She dropped the cup and watched the coffee spread across the top of the table and cascade to the floor.

Enzio reached for her arm and moved her to the next table. He set the box of chocolates down and signaled the waiter, ordered another sandwich and a sherry.

She watched the waiter sop up the spilled coffee and Enzio asked her what was wrong.

"It's nothing," she said.

She dabbed at the spots on her blouse with a napkin and tried to smile, to think of something amusing to say.

"Bringing chocolates to Switzerland?" she finally said. "Like coals to Newcastle?"

"Like fleas to Mesopotamia."

She succeeded in smiling at that. She wadded up the napkin and finished unwrapping the box.

She thanked him and offered him one.

"They're for you," he told her. "Chocolate is good for you. Gets your endorphins going, makes you happy."

She couldn't answer. Tears stung her eyes and she felt foolish.

"You missed me that much?" He offered the open box again. "An endorphin or two?"

The waiter brought the sandwich and the glass of sherry and set them down in front of Tamar.

"Drink your sherry and eat your chocolates," Enzio told her. "You need to think of something good." He took a chocolate from the box and handed it to her. "If you could think of something good, you can do anything, you can take flight and soar."

"Soaring is not what it's cracked up to be," she said. "I heard a story once about a little yellow bird who lived in a cage by a window." She lifted the chocolate and inspected it. "One day a skylark came by and saw the little yellow bird cooped up in the cage and felt sorry for her. 'Come with me, little bird,' he said, 'and we will soar above the clouds and into the great blue sky.' 'And in the great blue sky,' the yellow bird asked, 'is there a perch?'"

She popped the chocolate into her mouth. Enzio closed the box. He reached into his pocket for a packet wrapped in tissue and tied with a string.

"Another gift?" she asked.

"Not really." He unwrapped the tissue and put the spiral gold bracelet on the table between them.

She picked it up, examined the horse's head at one end and the coiled tail at the other. "The bracelet Gilberto gave me." She looked around for Herr Keller, not sure of what to do. "You stole it from my room. I called the police, you know."

"I got this from the police. It was in Demitrius' hotel room."

"Demitrius?"

Demitrius behind the splintered windshield. Demitrius trapped in a flooded car.

She tried a bite of sandwich. It was dry and tasteless, and stuck between her teeth.

"About Demitrius…" she began, then paused.

"They arrested him this afternoon," Enzio said.

He's alive.

"Demitrius stole the bracelet?" she asked. Somehow he got out of the car. "What made the police suspect him?"

"They were waiting for him on another matter."

"The accident?"

"Accident?"

"He skidded off the Mittlere Bridge into the Rhine," she said. Enzio raised his eyebrows and gave her a puzzled look.

"I'm not sure what happened," she said. "I only heard about it. Did he get out of the car before it sank?"

"Some swimmers pulled him out. The car is a total loss. When he got back to the Drei Konig, the police were waiting."

"They arrested him for skidding off the bridge?"

Enzio shook his head. "He's an accomplished forger and con artist. His real name is Dimitar Konstantinov."

"He's Bulgarian, not Greek?"

Enzio nodded. "He forges antiquities, whole collections." He pointed to the bracelet. "Like this bracelet from Chatham's collection of Thracian gold."

"And sells them for the real thing?"

"It's more complicated than that. What he would do was manufacture a whole collection, like the Bactrian hoard you saw at Gilberto's, using real gold. He and Irena would arrange for the collection to be exhibited, insured by a museum. They would steal it, collect the insurance, melt it down, and start all over with a new collection."

"How do you know?"

"We've been after him for some time."

"You and your mother?"

He smiled at that.

"Why did it take so long to arrest him?" she asked.

"We didn't have proof until now."

"The coin you stole?"

"Now we know the coin is modern. The bracelet may be too."

"How do you know?"

"We tested the coin."

"Your mother and you?"

He smiled at that again.

"Your mother lives in Lyon? What's her name?"

She waited for his answer. "Your mother gathers evidence to arrest people and she lives in Lyon where she has a lab. I think I know her name. She just moved to Lyon from Paris?"

"Yes," Enzio said.

"Because the food is better in Lyon?"

She took a bite of sandwich, then picked up the bracelet and examined it. "How can you tell if it's modern?" She looked closely at the finely chased finish. "It's made by the lost wax method, the same technique they used for ancient gold."

"We use a new test for authenticating archaeological gold, state of the art."

She turned the bracelet over in her hand. "What kind of test?"

"Archaeological gold contains uranium 238 as a trace element. With radioactive decay, the uranium produces helium. When the metal is heated to the melting point, all accumulated helium escapes and establishes a zero time for measuring when the artifact is manufactured. Accumulation of helium starts when the gold is cast and can be measured with a mass spectrometer."

"As a trace element? In parts per million?"

"Exactly."

"And the coin?"

"Not a bit of helium. Not even a trace. Not even 0.0001 in ppm—parts per million."

"So the coin is modern."

"Born yesterday," Enzio said.

"What about Irena?" Tamar asked. "Did the police arrest her too?"

"She's gone. The suitcase with the Bactrian hoard went with her. She's probably halfway to South America by now, looking for a new partner."

Tamar fingered the bracelet. "This bracelet was part of the Thracian gold that Chatham was taking to the British Museum?"

Enzio nodded.

"So Demitrius, or Dimitar, or whatever his name is, killed Chatham."

"Not likely," Enzio said. "When Demitrius saw you wearing the bracelet, he thought that you stole the Thracian gold."

"So he...."

"Tried to run you off the bridge. Gilberto said he got the bracelet from one of his runners. My guess is that something went wrong this time, someone else killed Chatham and found the gold after they killed him. A windfall."

Tamar took another bite of the sandwich and decided that she was hungrier than she thought. She signaled the waiter and asked for a menu.

"There's another reason that I don't think Demitrius killed Chatham," Enzio said. He leaned forward. "Orman Çelibi was killed in The Hague."

"Orman?" Tamar put down the sandwich. It tasted bitter.

"Two co-directors of Tepe Hazarfen have been killed," Enzio said. "You are the only one left."

This time, she spilled the sherry.

Chapter Twenty-Two

Basel, Switzerland, August 17, 1990

Tamar walked to Hohenstrasse through streets still damp from a nighttime drizzle and smelling of wet cement. Gilberto had told her to come by at ten o'clock, to wear comfortable shoes. He had smiled and rubbed his hands with anticipation and said, "You like Roman mosaics, no?"

A Mercedes limousine stood at the curb outside of Gilberto's house. The man she had seen at the basement door the other day leaned against the fender, smoking a cigarette. Today, he wore a gray chauffeur's uniform. Closer up, she saw that what she had thought was a sneer was a scar on the right side of his face that ran from his lip and across his cheek.

Before she could go up the walk, Gilberto appeared. He carried a picnic basket and led her to the limousine. With a bow and a grand gesture, he opened the door.

Inside, all gray leather and burled wood, Tamar sat in the back seat and stretched out her legs, luxuriating in the feel of the butter-soft leather against her back.

Gilberto sat next to her, placed the basket on the floor, clapped his hands, said, "I have a surprise for you," and grinned.

"A mosaic?" she asked, nursing a faint hope that he had found it.

"Better than that."

She aimed her foot at the basket. "We're going on a picnic?"

"Even better." He clasped her hand, leaned forward toward the driver and spoke to him in rapid Italian, saying something about Augst. Gilberto told the driver, as far as Tamar could make out, to take the route to Luzern and get off on exit eight. The driver said he knew the way.

"We're going to Luzern?" Tamar asked.

Gilberto, still holding onto her hand, gave her a bemused look. "You speak Italian?"

"I don't speak it. I understand a little."

He raised an eyebrow and smiled. "Of course. You know Latin. You translate Italian into Latin, and from there to English."

"Something like that. It makes for a thirty-second delay in processing," she said.

Gilberto raised her hand to his lips and kissed it. "Better than better." He chuckled and squeezed her hand again. "You'll see, you'll see."

Better than what? And where were they going?

They reached the highway, riding past suburban houses, and drove out into the open country.

"The driver is Italian?" Tamar asked.

"Swiss. He's from Ticino, from near Locarno on the Lago Maggiore. He grew up among pretty piazzas and colorful gardens in the shadow of the Castello Visconteo. It's a museum now." He squeezed her hand once more, as if there was a secret between them. "He's a romantic, and he dreams that he could be the illegitimate descendant of the Visconti Dukes of Milan."

"We all dream, don't we?" the driver rumbled from the front seat.

Tamar leaned toward Gilbert and said in a low voice, "I saw him coming out of the basement door a few days ago."

"Of course you did. He was probably making a delivery. He works for Helvetia Transport. I use them for shipping."

The Rhine flowed past on the left side of the highway. Gilberto gestured out the window with his free arm to the scattered meadows with an occasional cow or two and the pungent-sweet smell of pasture peeking through the trees of the wooded suburbs on the other side of the car.

"You know, of course, the story about how God made the meadows of Switzerland."

"I don't remember."

He laughed, and pressed Tamar's hand again. "When God made the world and everything in it, he asked the Swiss what they wanted. 'Give us some mountains,' said the Swiss." Gilberto pointed vaguely in the direction of the Juras in the distance, purple and gray through the mist. "So God gave them mountains. God saw that that was good, and asked the Swiss what else they wanted. 'Give us some meadows between the mountains', they said."

Gilberto dropped Tamar's hand to have both hands free to wave toward the meadows that nestled below the foothills and mountains of the Juras. "So God gave them meadows. God saw that that was good and asked what else the Swiss wanted. 'Give us some cows to put in the meadows,' they said. So God gave them cows. And God milked a cow, drank of the milk, and saw that it was good. 'What else do you want?' God asked. 'Three francs fifty-three,' the Swiss said."

Gilberto leaned back in the seat and laughed. Tamar laughed with him. He hadn't stopped smiling since they left Basel, and now he beamed as they pulled into a parking lot and stopped near a sign that said *Augusta Raurica*.

"This is Augst, oldest Roman city north of the Alps, with over 20,000 inhabitants in its heyday," he told her as the driver came around to open the back door. "Now we take a journey back in time, and it has taken less than fifteen minutes to get here."

Gilberto raised his eyebrows, and gave the driver half a nod. The driver nodded back, leaned against the trunk of the limousine and lit a cigarette.

"I've arranged a special treat," Gilberto told Tamar at the entrance to the site.

He traced his fingers on the map at the entrance along the paths that led to the *curia*, to the Roman house, and to the baths. "First, the cellar of the *curia*," he said at last, "the city hall."

He led her into a little museum with exhibit cases holding small figurines, silver statuettes of Roman gods and goddesses, iron tools, jewelry, and the characteristic fine Roman tableware of the first and second century AD—red Terra Sigillata.

Past the vitrines, they descended a few steps into what had been the basement of the *curia*. With a grand sweep of his arm, Gilberto presented the display—an array of mosaics.

"Over forty-seven mosaics were found here," he said. "From private houses and the baths, made from native materials—local limestone, glass, bits of broken ceramics. Most were simple geometric patterns, some with rosettes or vines." He pointed to a mosaic separate from the others, with the figure of a gladiator and, in the center, a crater with a fountain springing from it surrounded by fish. "This one, the gladiator mosaic, was found in the house of a rich man."

When a bell sounded from somewhere outside the *curia*, Gilberto grinned again.

"There it is," he said. "Now we go into the Roman world and live like Romans for just a little while."

He grabbed Tamar's hand, rushing toward the Roman house, pulling her along behind him as if she were a child. A guide met them at the entrance to the house. She said "*Ave*," in Latin, and led them to a changing room—a red-walled Roman bathing room with a small vitrine containing perfume bottles, a shelf piled with towels and togas, and an armless statue of Venus overlooking it all. The guide handed Gilberto a toga, Tamar a long tunic and peplos, and instructed them on how to dress as ancient Romans in simple Latin, illustrating her words with elaborate gestures.

She led them through the bathing process, all in Latin, showing them replicas of ancient bottles filled with oil that Romans used to anoint their bodies instead of soap, showing them the curved *strigilis* used for scraping off oil and residue as bathers prepared to plunge into the warm water of the *caldarium* before a quick, tingling dip into the cold water of the *frigidarium*. The guide reached for Tamar's arm, rubbed it with fragrant oil smelling of lavender and ran the *strigilis* against her skin, scraping away the remnant of oil.

They went on to the Roman house and, heads covered, paid homage to the *lares* and *larerium*—the household gods— ensconced in a niche in the colonnaded atrium, before they visited rooms with bright frescoed walls that led from the central court.

They went through a kitchen that had ceramic pans and casseroles stacked on shelves, pottery storage jars, wooden barrels, and brick ovens. A wax figure stood at a table making sausages.

Sausages and a kitchen for the staid Helvetii, Tamar thought. No Artemis for them, no Priapos. She pictured an ancient Swiss housewife bustling through the day, cooking and shopping and scrubbing the color off of frescoes.

They toured bedrooms and workrooms, and ended in the *triclinium*, the dining room, lined with long couches. Here, too, was a patterned mosaic floor. The contents of their picnic basket that Gilberto brought—eggs and olives, bread and cheese, and apples—were laid out on small tables set before the couches.

They began the meal. "*Ex ovo usque ad malum,*" the guide told them. From the egg to the apple, from the beginning to the end. As they ate, the guide made polite conversation in Latin, asking if they were well, if they enjoyed the house, if they enjoyed being Roman.

At the end of the tour, they removed the Roman costumes and emerged from the house into a different time and place, where children ran, and tourists moved along the paths examining and exclaiming over the strangeness of the ancient world.

"Now for the public baths," Gilberto said, taking Tamar's elbow. "There were hot springs here," he said. "For natural baths." He led her to the ruins of the baths next to the remains of the Forum, a hypocaust, where the square remnants of columns stood.

Tamar's vision of ancient Swiss captives of the Roman legions, forced to stoke the fires that heated the *caldarium* in the stifling basement of the baths, was interrupted by a loud exclamation, "*Defense de fumer.*"

Tamar turned to see a woman at the top of a small rise. The butt of the Frenchwoman's anger was a man standing near a small wooden box-like structure, calmly smoking a cigarette, gazing at something or someone in the other direction. The man looked like Enzio.

"I think Enzio is here," she told Gilberto.

"Not really? Where?"

When she turned back to show him, the man had disappeared.

Gilberto said, "Why would he be here, anyway?"

She could be mistaken, she thought, but still, she wondered why she saw Enzio when he wasn't there.

She asked Gilberto about the boxy structure near where the Frenchwoman had been standing.

"Those are the steps that lead to the sewer from the baths." He pointed to the knoll where the Frenchwoman stood. "The women's baths were there, near the entrance to the sewer. The tunnel is open to tourists."

"Let's go down the steps to the sewer," she said. "Let's explore."

"I'm too large for the tunnel. A sewer is the realm of rats. Not for the timid, or the tall." He hesitated. "If you must go down...."

But she had already started down the steps at the opening of the structure.

Gilberto was right, she thought, as she descended into the tunnel and slithered along dank stones smelling of mold toward the dark end of the sewer. The vault of the ceiling wept moisture a scant few inches above her head; the damp walls closed in on either side. She moved slowly, creeping along carefully, wary of slipping on the slick stones.

She thought she heard flat, masculine footsteps of someone who had entered the tunnel, hesitant at first and then surer, moving a little faster, a little louder, clattering just behind her, coming so close that she could smell the scent of stale tobacco on his clothing.

There was no room to let someone by. She was ready to turn around to apologize for blocking the way, to squeeze against the fetid walls to let him pass.

She had almost turned when the blow to the back of her head came and knocked her onto the cold stones.

When she opened her eyes outside, she was flat on the grass, with a headache and a thousand faces looking down at her, speaking German, speaking French, speaking Italian.

And Gilberto, looking concerned, carrying a package.

"What happened?" he asked.

She sat up. She felt dizzy and her head hurt even more. Two of the people that crowded around her helped her to her feet.

"I'm not sure. I think someone hit me."

He shook his head. "Too slippery. You slipped on the cobbles."

He paused awkwardly and held out the package. "I bought you some books in the museum shop."

Gilberto steadied her and she leaned against him. "It's time to go back to Basel," he said.

Back at the car, the driver leaned against the fender, smoking, looking the worse for wear. As she got into the limousine, Tamar noticed two buttons missing from his chauffeur's uniform and a black smudge on his sleeve.

Chapter Twenty-Three

Basel, Switzerland, August 18, 1990

Tamar took a taxi to Engelgasse 7 and rode the elevator to the seventh floor. Apartment 7A, Aristides had told her.

Her head still ached from yesterday's accident. Gilberto had insisted that it was an accident. "I told you not to go down there," he said in the car on the way back to Basel.

But she was sure that she had heard footsteps behind her, had smelled the remnants of cigarette smoke on someone's clothes.

A glass door etched with the figure of a peacock was opposite the elevator on the seventh floor. The handle appeared to be a large black snake. A brass plate engraved with the name Aristides and a small speaker were attached to the wall next to it.

Tamar pushed the button by the speaker.

A woman's voice came through. "*Wehr ist da?*"

"Dr. Saticoy," Tamar answered.

"Please to come in," the voice said.

A buzzer sounded, then a faint click. Tamar hesitated, not sure of what to do. She pulled on the snake-handle and the door opened.

Madame Aristides, with her perfect face and the big pearl on her finger, stood in a stark white anteroom with three translucent doors. She nodded in welcome and shook Tamar's hand, squeezing Tamar's fingers with the big pearl.

"You have an appointment with my husband, yes?" Madame Aristides moved her lips only slightly. "Please to follow me."

She opened one of the glass doors and led Tamar into a windowless room. A gilded peacock fountain bubbled in the center of a black and white ceramic tile floor laid out in concentric circles like an optical illusion.

The walls were painted in trompe l'oeil landscapes, each with a path leading through wooded hills and over a stream to a white spring. And on each path, a black snake.

Tamar stood transfixed, watching the water in the fountain play over the gold of the peacock against the backdrop of the dizzying floor.

Madame Aristides raised her hand to the painting on the far wall. The pearl on her finger glinted in the light. She pressed against the spot where the snake scuttled on the path and a door opened in the wall.

A magnetic latch, Tamar thought, and followed. Madame Aristides floated down a long hall. They continued past the open door of an office with books stacked on chairs and the floor and continued past a row of closed doors to a room at the far end of the hall.

Peacock feathers sprouted from large urns in each corner of the room. Two chairs and a polished coffee table faced a sofa.

Mustafa Yeğin, the man from Ankara, was seated on the sofa next to Leandro Aristides.

On his lapel, a pin with the metallic figure of a snake seemed to writhe and squirm as it caught the light when he turned to face her.

The men rose. Aristides bowed, offered a chair to Tamar, nodded his head in the direction of Mustafa and said, "The friend I was expecting from Turkey."

"We've met," Tamar said.

"In Turkey," Mustafa said. "At Hazarfen."

"You know about the missing mosaic?" Aristides asked.

With each move, Mustafa's snake seemed to glow and change color. "So you're Gilberto's American professor," he said. Tamar remained fascinated by Mustafa's snake.

Madame Aristides watched her, eyes narrowed. "The serpent is the ancient god of wisdom," she said and indicated the chair behind Tamar. "Please to sit."

Tamar landed in the chair still gazing at the scuttling snake, mesmerized by its luminous glimmer.

"You are fascinated by snakes?" Madame Aristides asked.

"She kills snakes," Mustafa said.

"You must never do that," Madame Aristides said as she slid into the other chair.

"The Great Goddess of the Minoans held a serpent in each hand to show she was the source of wisdom," Mustafa said.

Madame Aristides adjusted herself in her chair, and folded her hands.

Mustafa went on talking, telling Tamar that in Egypt, the serpent made the sap run and guarded the entrance to the underworld.

"The world of eternal life," he said, and talked of ancient Mesopotamia where a serpent guarded the tree of life, of the Garden of the Hesperides where it protected golden fruit. "Olympias," he told Tamar, "the mother of Alexander, was a snake handler, and Zeus came to her in the guise of a snake to father Alexander."

Tamar stirred uncomfortably in her chair and wondered if Mustafa was mad. He was still talking. "In Mesopotamia, Gilgamesh dove to the bottom of the waters to retrieve the plant of life."

The great pearl on Madame Aristides hand winked as she gestured for him to stop, but Mustafa went on talking. He told Tamar that a serpent came and ate the plant while Gilgamesh rested, and thus the serpent became immortal.

"So the serpent sheds its skin and each time comes forth glistening, fresh and renewed, always young."

Madame Aristide was visibly upset. Was he revealing some esoteric mystery that accounted for her implacable beauty? And what of the pearl, the huge pearl, that Madame Aristides had told Tamar that God created from his soul? The pearl looked like an enormous pustule to Tamar, and she involuntarily tightened her hold on the arms of her chair and tilted away from Madame Aristides.

"She's not interested in talk of the divine," Madame Aristides said to Mustafa.

"Divinity is like fire," Mustafa went on, "and like fire it has two faces."

Madame Aristides looked down and fingered the pearl.

"With one it gives light," Mustafa said, "with the other it harms and burns."

Tamar tried to turn the talk away from this and back to the mosaic. "Did you find out anything about the mosaic in Berlin?" she asked Mustafa.

"No sign there," he said. "Orman was supposed to be in Berlin. I left messages for him, but we couldn't connect. He never called me back."

"He was killed," Tamar told him.

Mustafa turned pale and threw up his hands in shock. "When? How?" He seemed like an actor straining for effect. "In Berlin?" His eyes remained intense, guarded.

"In The Hague."

"What was he doing there?"

"I don't know. But it's strange. First Binali, then Chatham, then Orman."

"What about Chatham?"

"You don't know? He was murdered in Bulgaria."

"What do you mean murdered? In Bulgaria? Why Bulgaria? He was going to visit his mother in Prague."

"You don't know about the Thracian gold? He was bringing it to the British Museum." Mustafa and Chatham were friends, for God's sake. They worked together at the British Museum. "It was in the news."

"I was traveling, didn't get to a newspaper."

"According to the papers, Chatham stopped in Sofia to examine a collection of Thracian gold that he heard about. He talked the collector into lending it to the British Museum."

"He was killed for the gold?"

"I thought so at first. Now with Orman killed too, I'm not so sure." She looked from Mustafa to Aristides. "You think their murders may be linked to the missing mosaic?" she asked them.

"No, no, not at all," Aristides said. "You are safe here in Basel. He thought for a moment and asked, "You know that Gilberto has a mosaic floor? Acquired recently."

"He told me it's from Italy." Tamar shrugged. "Not from Hazarfen."

"Did you see the mosaic?" Mustafa asked.

"It's in the warehouse, still being restored."

"Don't trust Gilberto," Mustafa said. "He's not what he seems."

"I'm aware of that."

"He's treacherous, more dangerous than you think."

Gilberto dangerous? Charming maybe, Tamar thought, devious, but treacherous? She was about to ask if he was as treacherous as a snake, then thought better of it.

Madame Aristides had been glancing at her watch while they were speaking, and now she looked at it again.

"You have to excuse us," she said to Tamar. "We have appointments at twelve o'clock. We must prepare. You will have to leave."

How rude. How abrupt.

Aristides responded to his wife's strange interruption by looking at his watch, as if she had given a signal. "Is it that late?" He stood up and turned to Tamar. "Sorry we couldn't help you."

"I understand," Tamar said, but she didn't. She got to her feet and Mustafa rose with her.

Aristides reached for Mustafa's arm. "You will stay, of course," he said to Mustafa, then extended his hand to Tamar for a farewell handshake. "My wife will see you to the door," he told her, and Madame Aristides led the way down the long hall, through the room with the peacock fountain, through the anteroom and to the elevator.

At the elevator, she hesitated. "You will excuse Mustafa. His parents were killed in a horrible manner when he was a boy. Today he was remembering."

"There's nothing to excuse." Tamar wondered at Madame Aristides' apology and her agitation at his long discussion of snakes. Was she also upset about what he said about Gilberto?

"Their bodies were mutilated in life and in death," Madame Aristides said. "People from the village could hear their cries all night. It was Mustafa who found them when dawn came."

She thought of the day when she heard of her parents' accident. "I understand," she said. The shock, the sadness, the loneliness that swept over Tamar that morning at her grandmother's house would always be with her. "I understand," she said again.

"No, you don't," Madame Aristides said and clicked the peacock door shut behind her.

Tamar watched her shadow fade behind the etched glass door and stared again at the handle like a serpent, and remembered Mustafa at Tepe Hazarfen, offended when she killed a snake.

Chapter Twenty-Four

Basel, Switzerland, August 18, 1990

They were just finishing lunch—the three of them, Gilberto, Enzio, and Tamar—seated around the glass table on the sun porch that overlooked the garden in the back of the house. In one corner of the room was the marble statue of a spear bearer—Greek or Roman, larger than life; against the wall, a false door plundered from an Egyptian tomb. They could hear Fabiana speaking in the kitchen. Her voice seemed low and musical, almost flirtatious.

They had been talking about the statue of the spear bearer, but all Tamar could think of was the fountain with the golden peacock and black snakes on the door handle at Aristides', painted on the walls, shimmering on Mustafa's lapel. What was it Orman said to Mustafa after she had killed the snake at Hazarfen? Devil worshipper, he had called him.

"It's probably a second-century copy of the Doryphoros," Gilberto was saying, gazing at the spear bearer, "the Canon, after Polycleitos."

"You know anything about Yedizi?" Tamar asked.

Gilberto looked startled, and a little annoyed at being interrupted. "A children's game? Why do you ask?"

"It has something to do with snakes."

"Yezidi?" Enzio said.

"That's it."

"It's a religious sect," Enzio said. "The Black Snake, left over from Mithraism, represents good men. Their chief deity is Malak Ta'us, the Peacock God, a fallen angel."

Tamar wondered whether to take a sip of wine. She put down the glass.

"What does Yezidi mean?"

Wine made her sleepy. Her head still hurt, just a little, dull, minor ache, and she had trouble keeping her eyes open.

"I'm not sure," Enzio said. "They claim the word Yezidi comes from Sumerian. Supposedly their religion is older than Zoroastrianism, Judaism, Christianity, and Islam. It has elements of all four, even Mithraism."

He spread his hands and shrugged. "It's a true syncretism—a mixture of Gnostic cosmology, ancient Pagan polytheism, Mithraism, with a little Islam and Christianity thrown in."

Gilberto poured another glass of wine and looked again toward the statue in the corner. "It was Polycleitos who set the standard for artistic beauty, established the canon for the symmetry and ideal proportions for the human body."

"Who and where was Yezidi founded?" Tamar asked. "Do they have a prophet?

Gilberto stood, refilled everyone's glass, and lifted his own. "To Polycleitos," he said.

Tamar looked at Enzio. "Do they?" she repeated.

"Some say that the founder is Yezid, the Umayyad Caliph. Some link it to Mithraism, some to Zoroastrianism, some even to the ancient Buzzard cult of Iraq and western Turkey."

"Like the buzzards drawn on the walls at Çatal Hüyük?" Tamar played with the stem of her wine glass. "Do they have anything on the Yezidi in the library at the university? Maybe some literature, sacred texts?"

"They have the Jelwa, or book of revelation. The Black Book, the Mishaf Resh, is an oral tradition. The story is that the original Mishaf Resh was stolen and is hidden somewhere in the basement of the British Museum."

"So someone might get a job in the British Museum to look for it."

"You're thinking of Chatham?"

She shook her head. "I'm thinking of Mustafa Yeğin. He's a friend of Chatham's."

Gilberto perked up. "Mustafa?" he asked. "You know Mustafa?"

"I met him in Turkey," Tamar said. "He's here in Basel now. I just saw him at Aristides'."

"Did you ask about my fresco?" Gilberto said.

"What fresco?"

"The one from the villa near Pompeii. I told you about it, showed you the photo." He moved uneasily in his chair. "It's over a year now." He rested his arms on the table. "He told me the fresco already left Italy by ship." He leaned forward, frowning. "According to Mustafa, the captain of the U.N. ship that patrols the Mediterranean took it aboard and brought it to Marseilles." He took a breath and a sip of wine. "Under the clandestine auspices of the U.N.," he said with a chuckle.

"A complicated route for a fresco," Enzio said. "Especially since there's no U.N. ship patrolling the Mediterranean."

"There must be. I paid Mustafa three hundred thousand dollars. Some of the money went to the U.N. captain."

"You're sure it was Mustafa *Yeğin*?" Tamar asked. "Mustafa is a common name."

"How is it supposed to get from Marseilles to here?" Enzio asked.

"That's easy." Gilberto spread his hands. "From there Mustafa picked it up by truck, smeared the license plate with mud to avoid detection, met another truck off the road to transfer the fresco, and crossed the border." He swiped his hands with a gesture of finality. "It should be here any day, may be here already."

Enzio reached for his glass, raised it to his lips, then changed his mind. "You paid Mustafa three hundred thousand dollars for a fresco that you have never seen and was never delivered?"

"You know nothing about business, Enzio." Gilberto shook his head. "My business is built on trust. If I can't take his word for it, I may as well quit." He took a sip of wine, banged the glass on the table and sloshed a little on the placemat.

Tamar watched Gilberto rub at the wine spill with his napkin. It couldn't be Mustafa, she thought, not Mustafa Yeğin, not Mustafa with the glimmering snake writhing on his lapel. The snake on the door handle, the fountain with the glittering peacock—the fallen angel—still stuck in her mind.

From the kitchen, a man's voice mingled with Fabiana's.

"Mustafa is here," Gilberto said, "with my fresco." He got up from the table and gulped down the rest of the wine in his glass. "Come," he said and headed for the kitchen.

Mustafa stood near the door, with Fabiana's head leaning against his chest as he clutched Fabiana's rump.

"She has something in her eye," Mustafa said.

Gilberto gave a humph and a smile. "I can see that." He turned to Tamar and Enzio. "You will excuse us?"

Tamar and Enzio waited in the salon. They sat in front of the Nineveh stele.

Tamar tapped her foot restlessly, troubled by what she had seen, troubled by Mustafa's duplicity. Enzio sat back and waited for her to speak.

"I don't understand," she said. "Gilberto really was talking about Mustafa. Gilberto said he bought a fresco from him."

"Does that surprise you?"

"He works for the Department of Antiquities in Turkey, and at the British Museum."

"And he shouldn't be doing this."

"And the thing with Fabiana and Mustafa. Does this happen often?"

"All too often. Fabiana is susceptible to…." Enzio smiled and waved his hands around while he searched for a word. "Sweet talk," he said. "Everyone knows it, and uses it to manipulate her."

"Why does Gilberto put up with it?"

"He feels he doesn't have much choice." He smiled again, and said with a conspiratorial whisper, "Fabiana was his first wife."

"He was married to Fabiana? For five years, I assume."

"Less than that. She was pregnant. She went away with her sister, gave birth to a nephew, and talked Gilberto into marrying her."

"He has a child?"

"It turned out the child wasn't his. Gilberto paid for his education anyway."

She tapped her foot again. "Are they devil worshippers?" she asked.

"Who?" Enzio asked.

"Yezidi?"

He shrugged. "Some say they are. For the Yezidi, the peacock is a beneficent deity, who was rehabilitated. But Moslems identify him with Lucifer, and they're convinced the Yezidi worship the devil."

"Do they have a Black Sabbath?"

"I doubt it. Very little is known of their rituals. No one has ever seen them worship. Lately though, they've begun to have more of a public presence. They have an autumn assembly when they sacrifice a bull, and a spring procession when they march with a bronze peacock—Malak Ta'us."

"The fallen angel?"

"Their worship centers around seven angels. The principal one is Malak Ta'us, the Peacock Angel. They don't worship evil. They're not Satanists."

"The Yezidi are from Turkey?"

"Turkey, mostly Iraq, Syria. Most of them are ethnic Kurds. There's even a large contingent in Europe. Germany, England, some even here in Switzerland."

"Like Aristides?"

"The peacocks and the snakes in his house? I suppose he might be, but he isn't very strict about it. They have a number of taboos he doesn't follow. His wife on the other hand—"

They heard the kitchen door close and Gilberto's footsteps coming toward them from the dining room, and they fell silent.

"Mustafa had to leave," Gilberto said.

"The fresco," Enzio asked. "Did he bring it?"

Gilberto shot him an angry look. "Still in transit."

Enzio paused, then looked at his watch. "I have to go. Have an appointment."

"Are you sure you can trust Mustafa?" Tamar asked after Enzio left. "Are you sure he will deliver the fresco?"

"Of course I'm sure. He's one of my runners. I deal with him all the time. I bought your bracelet from him. The fresco comes from the same villa near Pompeii where I got the mosaic floor."

"You bought the mosaic floor from Mustafa?"

Gilberto nodded.

"I would like to see it," Tamar said.

Chapter Twenty-Five

Basel, Switzerland, August 18, 1990

Enzio was in a hurry. He slammed the gate to Gilberto's house behind him, took the steps two at a time and rang the bell. That was when he saw Mustafa slip out the side entrance through the basement door while Enzio waited on the front steps for Fabiana to answer his ring. Mustafa scurried into the street without seeing him and snatched Enzio's waiting taxi.

When Fabiana finally opened the door, Enzio told her that he left his briefcase and rushed inside before she had time to tell him that she saw it on the table in the salon. She followed him inside.

"Gilberto isn't here?" he asked.

"He took the American professor to the warehouse."

"What was Mustafa doing here just now?"

"None of your business."

"Fabiana...."

She waved her hand in a vague way. "He wanted to see Gilberto about something."

"You told him where Gilberto went?"

"I said he was at the warehouse with the American professor. She wanted to see the mosaic."

"You told him that? That they went to the warehouse to see the mosaic?"

He rushed out, leaving Fabiana standing open-mouthed.

No taxi on Hohenstrasse. He dashed to the corner at Hard-strasse and started running toward the Rhine, looking for a taxi, afraid that he wouldn't reach the warehouse in time.

The warehouse was on the ground floor of an old building in Klein Basel. They stood in a large room, thirty by thirty feet across with doors that opened to smaller side rooms. A table in the center held bags of plaster, plastic containers streaked with dried plaster, brushes and pots of tempura paint in Pompeian red and gold. For the frescoes, Tamar thought.

"Your skin is like alabaster," Gilberto was saying, as he leaned toward Tamar.

Slabs of frescoes, looking like giant jigsaw puzzles, with pieces of the original stuck into a plaster matrix, were stacked against the corner near one of the doors. A sink stood against the far wall, and next to it, under a damp tarp, lay a hidden mosaic. Only the corner showed, white with plaster.

Gilberto leaned closer. "Has anyone ever told you—?"

"Never," Tamar said. "You're the first one."

Tamar could just make out the pattern of the corner of the mosaic—the familiar twisted guilloche, the cluster of fruit at the edge.

Gilberto drew closer, his breath rapid and heavy against her shoulder.

She started toward the far wall where the mosaic lay, leaving Gilberto canted at half-tilt. "This is the mosaic?"

He shifted his manner, smiling, expansive, businesslike. "You are fortunate. Objects like this don't come on the market very often."

He took a rag from the table, dampened it at the sink and threw back the tarp. He wiped the surface of the mosaic with the wet rag. The flowered vines still embraced the center medallion. The superb lady, worn and altered slightly by rough treatment but still enchanting, with a seductive gaze and a glow in her curved lips shimmering beneath the film of water.

Gilberto moved around to the front. "Beautiful, isn't it? But badly neglected. Needs restoration." He made a depreciating gesture toward the mosaic. "It was kept it in a shed in a country house, and lost tesserae here and there."

"You got it from Pompeii?"

"From France. It may have originally come from Pompeii, dug up in the last century. It was owned by an aristocratic French family who came on hard times."

"From the collection of the Marquis de Cuvier?"

"Exactly. The French family owned it since the late nineteenth century, 1890s. Before that, who knows?" He was right behind her now, his warm breath on the back of her neck. "I have a letter from the family attesting to the provenance."

She wanted to call him a liar, to let him know that she was on to him. She wanted to bargain over the price of the mosaic and let him get in deeper. She wanted to know where he got it, how it came here, who brought it, who took it from Tepe Hazarfen.

"This comes from Mustafa?"

He moved closer still, his body pressed against the curve of her back. "You could use it for your new museum, no? It could be a centerpiece, set the theme, be on display at the entrance."

She moved to the side and bent down as if to look more closely at the tesserae and almost lost her balance.

He took a deep breath and started again. "The price…. Well, there's what I paid for it and the expense of shipping and my costs for the restoration—I couldn't go below a million six."

Tamar stood up and moved back, as if she were taking in an overall view of the mosaic. "That's a little high. I don't think I could get the trustees to come up with more than a million. Eight hundred thousand, more likely."

"This is not a flea market, Miss Saticoy."

"Dr. Saticoy," she said, and tilted her head as if thinking. "I would need a full provenance before I could bring it to the trustees."

"Of course, my dear," he said. "I stand behind any object I sell. The only way to keep my reputation for honesty and fair dealing." He leaned toward her again. "Ask anyone in the business, my dear, anyone." He smiled his charmed smile and lifted an eyebrow. "I have the bill of sale from the French family. Along with the letter."

"And where is it really from?"

He moved his shoulders and drew out his hands in a gesture of explanation. "It could be Late Roman provincial from somewhere in the Eastern Empire. Turkey, perhaps."

"He's right, you know," said a voice from the doorway. "It's from Turkey."

Mustafa stood at the entrance, and he was pointing a gun at them.

Chapter Twenty-Six

Basel, Switzerland, August 18, 1990

Mustafa waved the gun vaguely in the air in the direction of the mosaic. "From Tepe Hazarfen." The weapon, matte and dark gray, looked heavy and trailed after his hand like an extra appendage.

"You were looking for the mosaic, yes?" he asked Tamar and aimed the gun at them.

"The gun isn't necessary," Gilberto said in a low, wary voice. "Put it away." He held out his hands and took a step forward. "Then we can talk."

"Nothing to talk about." The gun trembled at the end of Mustafa's outstretched arm. "It's done," he said, and his hand steadied.

Tamar backed away. Will he really shoot?

A distraction, we need a distraction.

She looked around the room for something to hide behind, something to use, some way to stop him, saw the paint jars on the table and moved toward them.

She began talking slowly, carefully. "Gilberto said he got the mosaic from you. Did he?"

"I'm his connection, his runner."

She glanced at the table, moved a little closer. "You stole it from Hazarfen?"

He brought up his other hand to steady the gun and for a moment held it with both hands.

She took another step toward the table. Slowly, slowly. Don't make it too obvious.

"How did you know the mosaic was there? I didn't tell you about it until the morning you came for the divisions."

"Put the gun away," Gilberto said again, and Mustafa brandished it in the direction of Gilberto.

Talking won't help, Tamar thought. Mustafa won't put the weapon away; he means to use it.

"Chatham? Was it Chatham?" she asked.

Mustafa's hand was steadier, the gun pointed at Gilberto. "He was my partner. He was too greedy. He'd do anything for money."

"And you won't?" Gilberto said, moving toward Tamar.

She wanted to say: don't make him angrier. She wanted to say: stay where you are, so he has two targets. She wanted to say: keep him distracted.

"Put the gun away," Gilberto repeated.

"Gilberto told me he got the gold bracelet from you," she said. "You got the bracelet from Chatham, didn't you?" She moved another step toward the table. "You killed Chatham and took the Thracian gold."

"He was killed in Bulgaria." He trained the gun on her. "I was never there."

She shifted closer to the table. Gilberto moved with her. She signaled to Gilberto to keep his distance. He didn't notice, stayed close.

"Orman," she said. "You killed Orman, too."

He glanced toward the mosaic then leveled the gun at her. His hand was steady now. "I didn't kill him." He shrugged. "Maybe he was greedy, too. Maybe he wanted more than his share for the mosaic, more than Chatham."

"You're lying," she said. "Orman wouldn't steal from the site."

"How do you know?"

She shifted closer to the table. "How much did Gilberto pay you for the mosaic?"

Another shuffle toward the table, with Gilberto following. He's trying to shield me, she thought.

"You stole four hundred thousand dollars from Gilberto," she said. Another step toward the table. "You charged him for a fresco that wasn't there."

"He owed me."

She was nearly at the jar of paint. "Stealing is stealing. Gilberto trusted you. I trusted you."

"What good is trust? We need the money."

"Who's *we*?"

He shook his head and waved the gun again. "You don't understand. With money we can organize, train like soldiers, choose targets that the world will notice. We can do something, find a way to fight back, to stop the humiliation and persecution."

She was at the table now, her hand crawling toward the tempura, reaching for the jar, and Mustafa was watching her.

"First we need the money," he said. He stopped, gestured at her with the gun. "Get away from the table." He brought up the gun and pointed it, holding it with both hands at arm's length. "You think you can kill me like you kill a snake?" he asked. "With a pot of paint instead of a stone?" and he aimed.

A bright flash discharged from Mustafa's hand just as she grabbed the jar and hurled it. An explosion filled the room, echoed into silence that stung her ears.

She saw paint splatter over Mustafa's hand and arm, heard the gun clatter to the cement floor.

She saw Mustafa rub yellow paint across his forehead, felt the weight of Gilberto fall against her, shivered as Gilberto dropped to the floor, thinking as he fell, he tried to save me.

She saw Enzio and the detective with the leather trench coat at the door, saw them hurl Mustafa to the ground, saw them handcuff him.

She knelt beside Gilberto. "You'll be all right," she told him.

She took his hand, stroked his arm.

"You'll be all right," she repeated, but she knew he wouldn't.

She heard sirens bleat in the distance, coming nearer. An ambulance?

"You'll be all right," she said to Gilberto again.

She watched the trickle of blood from his mouth and nose, felt him gasp for breath through the pink foam of bubbles at his nostrils and the corners of his mouth.

"You'll be all right," she said.

Gilberto stopped wheezing, stopped bleeding.

"You see," Tamar said, "I told you, you'd be all right. You're not bleeding any more."

The siren grew louder.

Enzio stood next to her. "Come away, Tamar," he was saying.

The froth at Gilberto's nose and mouth had burst and ran down in tiny rivulets along his cheeks. She wiped them off with her sleeve and he didn't stir.

She heard the rumble and whine of the ambulance stop outside the warehouse door, heard doors slam, heard the scurry of feet, heard voices call.

"The ambulance is here," she said to Gilberto.

"Come away, Tamar," Enzio said. "There's nothing you can do."

Gilberto's face softened and was still. "I told you, it would be all right," she said again and felt Enzio's hand on her shoulder.

Gilberto's gaze was unblinking, without expression.

"His eyes," she said. "Look at his eyes."

Gilberto stared, his pupils so dilated that he seemed to have no iris.

"It's as though he walked into a dark room," she said.

"Yes, Tamar," Enzio said. He cupped his hand beneath her elbow and helped her to her feet. "A very dark room."

Chapter Twenty-Seven

Basel, Switzerland, August 19, 1990

"You'll feel better after you drink it," Enzio had told her when he ordered grappa for her.

Feel better? After yesterday? After Gilberto's unblinking eyes stared at her? After her interview with the police that went on and on?

She lived through it again and again, the moment always the same: the flare from the muzzle of the gun, the blast of the gunshot reverberating through the warehouse, the splatter of paint on Mustafa's arm, Gilberto falling against her.

Tamar and Enzio sat at an outside table in the dappled sunshine at the bottom of the Freiestrasse, picking at their food, Enzio toying with pesto, Tamar looking down at a shrimp salad. They were waiting for the *Herald Tribune* to be delivered to the kiosk next door. Neither one spoke.

Yesterday she had given the deposition to Herr Fischer, the detective with the leather trench coat. Seated across from his desk in the police station, she repeated it again and again, told him what had happened, while he stopped and started the tape recorder that logged the interview.

Without his trench coat, wearing a dark polo shirt with an open collar, he sat back in his chair and played the stop button on the tape recorder like a pianist at a concert, with an arched finger and a flourish.

He had stopped and started the machine three times. Once, he got up to adjust the window shade, the next time to turn on the rotating fan that stood near the window, and then to turn off the fan and rearrange the papers on the shelves behind him that had been blown out of place.

Each time he started her from the beginning. He asked her to repeat what had happened, nodded his head in encouragement. She would begin again, and tell him about seeing the flash from the gun, hearing the explosion, seeing the splatter of paint on Mustafa's hand and shirt, feeling Gilberto fall against her.

And he would ask, "The gun fell to the ground after the pot of paint hit him?"

She would say yes, and repeat it again.

Over and over, until she felt nothing, until she could tell it by rote and the pain was almost gone.

Tamar tried another sip of grappa. Her hand shook as she lifted the glass, and a few drops landed on the table.

She put the glass down again. "It tastes awful."

"It's supposed to. It's medicinal."

She fingered the card in her pocket that Fischer had given her with his number, and thought of his admonition to call him in case. In case what? He had never finished the sentence.

"I kept telling him," she said to Enzio and reached for a napkin to wipe up the spill. "The flash from the gun, the blast of the gunfire, the paint on Mustafa's hand, on Mustafa's sleeve, then Gilberto falling. And Fischer kept asking."

"Mustafa claims it was an accident," Enzio said. "He says that the gun went off when he dropped it after you hit him with the paint."

"He said that?" Tamar closed her eyes and sank in her chair. "Then Mustafa didn't kill him. It was me." Tears began to form beneath her closed lids. "I killed Gilberto."

"But that's not what happened," Enzio said.

The tears coursed down her cheeks. "What then?" She couldn't stop the tears from coming, and felt foolish.

"Mustafa fired before the paint pot hit him," he said. "You remembered the right sequence. The gunshot, the paint on his hand, Gilberto falling."

"You think?"

"Gunshot residue from firing the gun was under the paint on his hand." Enzio forked some pesto. "Paint overlaid the flashback residue on his sleeve." He paused and leaned forward. "Fischer just needed corroboration," he said with intensity.

"You're sure Mustafa fired before the paint hit him?"

He nodded and twisted the forkful of linguine around on the edge of his plate. "Even if Mustafa's cleared for Gilberto's murder, he still has to be extradited to Turkey for antiquity theft. The mosaic isn't the only thing he stole from archaeological sites."

"The Kybele?"

"The one in the Marquis de Cuvier collection."

"Gilberto knew."

"The shooting was no accident," Enzio said. "Gilberto was his target."

"Why would he do that? Why would he kill Gilberto? Was it about the fresco that never arrived? The four hundred thousand dollars? Gilberto demanded his money back?"

Enzio shrugged, and held out his hands in a questioning gesture.

"What happened to the money?" she asked.

"It's long gone."

"Mustafa stashed it in a numbered account?"

"Better than that. He used it to buy arms. It disappeared into the hawala system."

"Hawala?"

"An old system used in the Middle East to hide transactions. Mostly, it's used to evade taxes, but it's perfect for any illegal activity—terrorism, smuggling. Hundreds of thousands of dollars can be exchanged with just a telephone call. It predates modern banking, probably the ancestor of western banking."

Another gift of the Crusades, Tamar thought, like scallions and castles with crenellated turrets, like games such as hazards, and like the revival of learning.

"Money or its equivalent is moved through brokers," Enzio said. "Hawala means to change or transform."

"And the money just disappears?"

"It works like letters of credit," Enzio said. "Or checks, for that matter. Most often, credit, not money moves through the system. No records, no paperwork, and no one is the wiser. Cash is paid in at one end, the hawala broker charges two percent, and credit is passed along. Eventually, money comes out at the other end without a bank or a paper trail. No taxes, no official exchange rate. Everyone gains. Government officials can hide bribes, gangsters can hide loot, terrorists can hide funding. The system helps everyone, and everyone does well by doing good."

"Is it legal?"

"It's a kind of black market."

"Why would any government stand for it?"

"Most of the money comes from legitimate sources—'white hawala.' It's used to transfer money earned by 'guest workers' back to their home village, just small amounts every month. When you add it all up it contributes a lot to the economy of the third world, so they turn a blind eye. It's the 'black hawala' that's connected to illegal activities and money laundering, siphoned off to terrorists to buy arms, explosives, to support them while they train. Sometimes it's used in the drug trade."

"All *sub rosa*."

"Hawala can turn goods into cash, cash into goods. Anything of value that can be shipped, smuggled, turned into dollars. Goods are as good as cash. What the Middle East has in quantity—antiquities—or diamonds, gold."

"Gold?" she asked. She speared a shrimp with her fork and waved it in the air. "Like Demitrius' gold? The Thracian gold, the Bactrian hoard?"

"Yes, that kind of gold."

She narrowed her eyes and put down her fork. "Gilberto was in the middle of it," she said finally. "Demitrius brought the Bactrian hoard to him. Gilberto had the Thracian bracelet. He said he got it from Mustafa, but Gilberto gave it to me before Mustafa arrived in Basel."

"He didn't get it from Demitrius. Demitrius and Irena came here looking for it. He may have gotten it from Mario."

"Who's Mario?"

"Fabiana's friend. You remember, the man she gave the deposition about?"

They fell back into silence, into looking down at their food and picking at it.

"What is the Marquis de Cuvier collection?" she asked after a while.

Enzio smiled and held out both hands in explanation. "Another of Gilberto's inventions. He had letterheads made with a crest of the fictitious Marquis. To give items a credible provenance, he would age his correspondence from the Marquis in the oven and dab the pages with used teabags."

"Wouldn't it be obvious?"

"It fooled you."

"What did Mustafa mean when he said 'It's done' to Gilberto before he shot him?" Tamar said after a while.

"He said that?"

Tamar nodded.

"The four hundred thousand dollars Gilberto gave Mustafa must have been for something else, not for the fresco."

"You remember?" she asked. "We said that whoever took the Thracian gold killed Chatham? Gilberto ended up with some of it."

"So far, we only know about the bracelet. You think Gilberto had something to do with Chatham's death?"

She didn't want it to be true. "I don't know." But too much pointed to Gilberto's complicity. "What else goes through the hawala system?"

"Besides antiquities and gold? Any kind of contraband, even a little heroin."

"Heroin?"

"It's lightweight, it pays well, it can fit in the hollow of a statue, so it can be smuggled along with antiquities inside an artifact."

"You think Gilberto dealt in heroin?"

Enzio shook his head. "Not Gilberto. He was too smart." He thought about it a moment. "And Gilberto was too smart to raise questions by getting involved in a murder." He paused and leaned back in his chair. "Gilberto had a runner in the Netherlands, brought in some antiquities through a circuitous route."

"And something else with it? From Amsterdam?"

"Amsterdam is too obvious. He's cleverer than that. His contact is in The Hague."

"The Hague is where Orman was killed."

"Exactly," Enzio said.

Chapter Twenty-Eight

Basel, Switzerland, August 19, 1990

"Now that we found the mosaic," Tamar said, "I should go back to California." She speared another shrimp and a piece of tomato with her fork. "I have to get ready for my classes. They start in a few weeks."

With the sun pleasantly warm on her back, with shoppers strolling along Freiestrasse, Tamar didn't want to know the truth about Gilberto, didn't want to know that Orman was dead, or that Mustafa had killed Gilberto. She wanted to push a magical rewind button and go back to before yesterday.

And then she remembered her purse.

She had left it behind when she and Gilberto left for the warehouse.

"I may have to get a new passport," she said. "It's in my purse. I left it at Gilberto's."

"The house isn't closed," Enzio said. "Fabiana is still there. You could go back and get it. You want me to go with you?"

"I'm a big girl now. I can take care of myself." She put down her fork. "Fabiana hasn't left for Cortina?"

"She may stay in Basel a while. Gilberto willed the house and furnishings to the fellow she called her nephew. Name is Benito Motti."

"Furnishings? Does that include the antiquities?"

"According to his solicitor." He shrugged.

"How do you know all this?"

"Fischer checked the will. Gilberto left each of his other wives one hundred thousand dollars," he added, then he laughed. "If you had married him—"

"I could be rich beyond my wildest dreams. What about the goods in the warehouse? Does that go to the so-called nephew, too?"

"I'm not sure. We have to look into what's stored there, check what's legal and illegal. The mosaic may not be the only stolen item." He paused and busied himself with winding linguine on his fork. "And then there's the question of illicit export. He may have paid for things like frescoes, but Italy can claim anything that's cultural property, illegal to export."

"Museums can't buy cultural property or deal in stolen pieces. Even private parties can get arrested. Didn't a museum get into trouble over something from Italy a few years ago?"

"The dealer did. Then he bribed some Italian officials and it all went away."

"And Gilberto? What would he have done with the mosaic?"

"Probably sell it to the Getty. They have money to throw around."

"As another piece from the Marquis de Cuvier collection?"

"Probably." His fork dangled in midair with strands of linguine trailing onto his plate. "He would have found a way." He dropped the fork and sighed. "It's too depressing. I want to finish this and go back to my day job."

"Your day job? I thought you worked for Interpol."

"Only on a contract basis, as a consultant. Interpol has a list of people they call on, experts they call us, for specific jobs. I have a contract for this job. They pay well. You would be good at it, you know."

"What is your day job?"

"I'm the Keeper of Ancient Art at the Museo Archeologico Nazionale in Naples. I specialize in mosaics—Pompeiian, mostly."

"I should have guessed," she said and frowned. "You know too much about archaeology." She toyed with the shrimp, then leaned back in her chair. "You get time off from the museum to work for Interpol?"

"They clear it with the Director of the Museum. He fabricates some excuse for me to leave—sometimes a research grant, sometimes fieldwork." Picked up his fork again and rolled more strands of linguine around it. "He's the only one who knows I work as a consultant for Interpol. Now you know too." He waved the loaded fork in a vague gesture. "I think Gilberto suspected it."

"He didn't do anything about it."

"I think he liked the challenge."

She waited for him to take a bite of pasta or put down the fork. He did neither, just contemplated her with the fork suspended in midair.

"They're going to contact you, you know," he said. "I recommended you, told them how you worked with us. They need a replacement for Orman."

"Who?"

"Interpol."

"A university isn't the same as a museum. We have a schedule of classes. I don't think I could get away."

"Orman managed it. Interpol could arrange things with your dean." He still held the fork in the air. Some loose pieces of linguine looked dangerously close to falling on the table. "It pays exceptionally well."

Tamar stabbed at another shrimp, then pushed her plate away. "I'm not very hungry," she said.

Enzio raised his eyebrow and said, "You need something to rouse your endorphins."

He finally put down the fork and shoved his plate to the side. He summoned the waiter and ordered a Coupe Danois for Tamar and a Coupe Framboise for himself. The waiter cleared the table.

"What did you order?" she asked after he left.

"Gelato. A hot fudge sundae laced with Grand Marnier for you. Mine has a Cointreau-raspberry sauce."

"Guaranteed to awaken endorphins?"

He nodded and smiled at her.

The gelato, topped with whipped cream, came in tulip glasses with long-handled dessert spoons. Tamar's had a small pitcher of chocolate sauce on the side that she poured over the gelato. It hardened slightly, then floated on the softening ice cream.

She tried a spoonful, felt it melt on her tongue, savored the luxury of chocolate and cream with the bite of orange brandy.

"Magnificent," she said, and took another spoonful.

Enzio lifted his spoon, arched it over to her plate and dipped into the tulip glass for a dollop of the Coupe Danois. He tasted it, licked the spoon, took another spoonful, and smiled.

"Definitely a magnificent moment," he said.

He poured the raspberry sauce over his gelato and, grinning, fed a spoonful to Tamar. She savored the bright flavor of warm raspberries, the rich taste of vanilla ice cream, the soft tang of Cointreau, and reached over to the Coupe Framboise for another spoonful. She rolled it on her tongue to appreciate the full flavor before she swallowed it, then tried the chocolate coupe again and threw back her head and laughed.

She dipped into it again. When the soft ice cream spilled on her dress, she laughed, and laughed again when Enzio dropped a spoonful on his shirt.

They continued this way, spoons across the table flashing in the sun, laughing all the time, dipping into each other's servings, smiling into each other's eyes, lips shining, sticky with chocolate and raspberry.

They scraped the last few drops of sauce from the bottom of their dishes, licked the spoons, and leaned back, still laughing.

"I'm all endorphined out," Tamar said after a while, and they still sat, looking at each other and smiling until a truck pulled up to the kiosk next door and the driver tossed a stack of newspapers tied with a cord on the curb in front of the kiosk.

Enzio said, "Today's *Tribune*." He braced both hands on the table, stood up and started next door to the kiosk.

176 Aileen G. Baron

Tamar signaled the waiter for a bottle of Evian water. He had just cleared the remains of the gelato and wiped the table when Enzio returned. Enzio pushed aside the chairs, moved the glasses, and spread the paper on the table.

There on the front page below the fold, the headline read *NOTED ART DEALER MURDERED IN BASEL.*

They stood side by side to read it. The story said that Mustafa Yeğin, Turkish archaeologist, was being held as Gilberto's alleged killer. It continued on an inside page with a paean to Gilberto as an outstanding antiquities expert and art dealer.

Two columns over, another a story with the heading *SMUG-GLER ARRESTED FOR MURDER OF ARCHAEOLOGIST* with a dateline from The Hague grabbed Tamar's attention. The article, only three paragraphs long, said that Mario Firenzano, recently released from a Turkish prison for trying to smuggle out hashish hidden in an ancient figurine, had been extradited from Basel and was accused of the murder of Orman Çelibi in The Hague.

"Mario Firenzano," Tamar repeated. The name sounded vaguely familiar. "Is that the Mario you meant? Fabiana's friend? The one she gave the deposition for that first day I went to Gilberto's? I remember. They had to let him go."

Enzio looked up at her. "He was one of Gilberto's runners."

"I remember. Gilberto said he stole some coins. Why would he risk dealing with Gilberto by stealing something as minor as coins?"

"The coins were a payment to Firenzano. That's why the window was left open. Firenzano gets paid. Gilberto gets the money back from the insurance company to cover the robbery."

"So that's why Gilberto called the police and reported the robbery? For the insurance?"

"I don't think it's as simple as that. I'm not sure how much Gilberto knew."

"That Fabiana was paying Firenzano off?"

"The extent of it."

"I think I met Firenzano. What does he look like?"

"He's easy to spot. Has a scar that runs from his eye to the corner of his lip."

"Makes it look like he's sneering?"

Enzio nodded his head. "It does look like that."

"He's stocky, with curly gray hair and large liquid eyes?"

"You've seen him here, in Basel?"

"He drove us to Augst. And before that, I saw him leaving Gilberto's by the basement door."

"When you saw him, was that before or after Gilberto gave you the bracelet?"

She tilted her head in thought and sat down. "You think Firenzano could be the one who brought it from Bulgaria." She closed her eyes and tried to remember. She got out of the taxi the day she saw him at the basement door, and told Gilberto about it. A friend of Fabiana's, Gilberto had said, and then Enzio showed up.

"The day you came with the *oinichoe*," she told him.

"Firenzano had just arrived from Bulgaria that day. He stopped at Gilberto's before he went to The Hague."

"The bracelet came from Firenzano? He brought it to Gilberto?"

Enzio folded the paper and sat down next to her. "Looks like it. Firenzano killed Binali Gul, killed Orman, killed Chatham, and he was after you when he showed up at Gilberto's. He came after you in the tunnel at Augst."

Tamar rubbed her forehead, dropped her hands in her lap, and looked down at them. "You were in Augst too, I saw you."

"I followed him in, and we tussled. I carried you out and put you on the grass." He smiled. "The fireman's lift. It wasn't easy. I had to walk bent over, lugging a heavy weight through that narrow tunnel."

"You didn't arrest him?"

"It doesn't work like that. I can't arrest anyone. I'm a consultant, just do investigations and report to the local police. I called Fischer. He had Firenzano picked up and extradited to The Hague."

Tamar played with her fingers, bending them to form a pagoda, closed them into a fist and lined up her thumbs side by side. "I thought maybe you were the one who knocked me on the head."

"I saved you. I carried you out with rats from the tunnel clutching at my pants leg." He leaned forward and stroked her arm. "Ah, the things I do for you." He sat back and gazed at her fondly, then said with a frown, "We have to face it. Wherever we look, everything points to Gilberto."

She reached for the water and took a long gulp. "I don't think so. He didn't know it was going to happen."

"Gilberto wasn't running the whole thing," Enzio said.

She thought of Mustafa's words, 'It's done,' thought of Demitrius coming to Gilberto when he was looking for the Thracian gold. But Gilberto bought books for her in Augst. He expected her to come out of the tunnel alive.

"He wasn't responsible for what happened in Augst," she said. "Gilberto may have been wheeling and dealing in antiquities. But someone else was running Gilberto."

Chapter Twenty-Nine

Basel, Switzerland, August 19, 1990

Tamar pushed the bell again and kept her finger on the button until she saw someone, not Fabiana, descend the red carpet to the door. Tamar could make out just trouser legs and soft Italian shoes through the beveled glass.

A man with brown curly hair tumbling over his forehead and bright amber eyes opened the door. She had never seen him before.

"Herr Dela Barcolo isn't here," he said with a soft Italian accent.

"I'm aware of that," she said and paused, not sure of what to say next.

He looked like a real estate agent. He wore gray slacks, a blue blazer, and a tie.

"I can show you what you want to see in the absence of Signor Dela Barcolo," he said at last. "I know the collection." He stood aside and made a welcoming gesture in the direction of the foyer. "Please to come in."

He led her past the vitrines of the foyer, past the staircase. "You wish to see something of classical Greek, no?"

She was ready to answer, to say that she only came to collect her purse, but she let him go on.

"I will show you the work of a master," he said. "If you see it, you will want it." They passed the salon. "No need to buy now, you must think about it, taste it with your mind." They continued into the dining room, where he skirted the enormous table, today piled with books and ledgers.

"I am Ercole Sforza," he said.

His foot felt along the floor, and Tamar realized he was searching for the button to open the cabinets on the far side of the room.

"Sforza?" she said. "Like the medieval Dukes of Milano?"

His foot wandered back and forth beneath the table. "I can only dream." His voice strained from the exertion of probing for the button. "The name is Sforza, and I am from Milano. Alas, from the wrong side of the blanket."

He found the button at last and waved his arm in a dramatic gesture as if he were performing a magic act. The cabinets opened and he glided over to the far wall and reached for a *kylix*.

He held it out to her. "You see. It is signed Epiktetus," he said, and turned it over.

"With a flute player and dancer in the tondo," she said, remembering. "It's beautiful."

"But not so beautiful as you. Your eyes are magic. You have held many a man captive with your eyes."

His voice was low and intimate but his delivery was not as good as Gilberto's. Tamar wondered what would come next, when Fabiana's strident voice came from the doorway.

"What do you want here?"

Fabiana advanced into the room, all the while railing in rapid Italian at Sforza. She called him Benito. As far as Tamar could make out, Fabiana told Benito to leave, that she would take care of everything. He reddened, then shrugged, and left through the kitchen.

"Why are you here?" Fabiana asked Tamar.

She crossed the room and shoved the doors of the cabinet closed until they clicked and turned back to Tamar. "You haven't made enough damage? You destroyed Gilberto. If it weren't for you...." Her face was red and the veins of her neck stood out. "And now you're after me and Benito."

"I came for my purse," Tamar said.

"You think I stole it? It's locked in the desk upstairs. Everything is safe, just as you left it, your purse, your wallet, your passport. You think I need your money?" She said all of it quickly, without stopping.

"I left it yesterday—" Tamar began, but Fabiana had already started for the stairway.

Tamar followed.

"The young man," Tamar said. "You called him Benito?"

"He's my nephew."

"Benito Motti?"

Fabiana's grip on the banister tightened so that her knuckles stood out. "Yes. My nephew," she said again.

"From Cortina?" Tamar climbed the next step. "He told me his name was Ercole Sforza."

"He changed it." Fabiana turned around and looked down at her. "He studied at the university in Florence," she said, as if that accounted for a new name.

And maybe it did, Tamar thought. When Gilberto was Sergio Benetti, he was a street lout in an ill-fitting suit, but as Gilberto Dela Barcolo, he could charm the sweat off a horse. Sergio Benetti married Fabiana. Gilberto Dela Barcolo married a rich American widow and sold antiquities on Madison Avenue.

Benito Motti is just a peasant boy from a village in the Alps. Ercole Sforza can walk with princes—princes and thieves. And Fabiana can teach him how, just as she probably taught Gilberto.

Gilberto and Ercole are creations of Fabiana, just as Firenzano was. It was Firenzano who sneaked through the basement window that Fabiana had left open when the coins were stolen from Gilberto. It was Firenzano Tamar saw at the basement door after he met with Fabiana, Firenzano who brought the Thracian gold from Bulgaria.

Fabiana continued up the stairs toward the gallery. Tamar trudged after her, uncertain whether to follow.

Fabiana couldn't have run it all—run Gilberto, run Firenzano, run smuggling contraband, run stealing finds from archaeological sites that ended up in Basel.

They had reached the landing now. The vitrine stood against the far wall just as it had before, but the desk had been moved closer to the railing into a dark corner of the gallery. The Kore stood alone on its plinth near the corner of the gallery.

Light filtered from the skylight and glanced off the glass door of the vitrine. Tamar noticed gaps in the shelves; the place where the Roman Kybele had been was empty. The Kybele was gone.

Fabiana grunted and pointed to left lower drawer of the desk. "In there," she said.

Tamar had to wedge herself into the narrow space between the desk and the railing to open the drawer.

The drawer was stuck. She tugged again. It pulled loose, she stumbled against the rail, the purse fell to the floor.

She reached for it. No room to bend. She kicked at it with her foot, pulled it up by the handle.

Fabiana had moved to the front of the desk, crowding Tamar into the corner next to the Kore. Tamar tried to wriggle past. Fabiana blocked the way.

Fabiana reached into the top drawer of the desk, took out a packet wrapped in blue tissue paper and began to unwrap it, rolling the paper along the top of the desk.

"This dagger belonged to an Arab sheik in the time of the Crusades," Fabiana said without blinking. "Gilberto has a buyer who will pay a million dollars for it."

A diamond hilted dagger with a gold blade rolled out of the wrapping and across the desk.

Gold is too soft to do any harm, Tamar thought. It's just decorative.

"Beautiful," she said.

Fabiana picked up the dagger, wrapped her hand around the hilt, and jabbed it in the air. Her face was blank and cold, with no expression—no acknowledgment, no rage, no warning.

Tamar felt a chill of fear, her pulse quickened; she backed further into the corner. The purse swung awkwardly from her shoulder. She squirmed in the narrow space, tried to get around Fabiana.

Fabiana lurched forward, the dagger clutched in her fist, pointed at Tamar.

Tamar ducked. The tip caught her right arm.

"Just decorative," Tamar said.

She looked down. Her arm was bleeding.

She tried to move out, swung the purse. Fabiana ducked, pressed closer and let loose a rapid spate of Italian.

Tamar's arm throbbed.

"Gold over steel," Fabiana said and fingered the tip of the blade. "Like me."

Her grip tightened on the handle of the blade. "It was used for royal executions."

She lunged, thrust the dagger at Tamar.

Tamar dodged. It caught her on the side, rent her dress, nicked her arm again.

She shrank back, wedged tighter into the corner, held the purse in front of her like a shield.

"It's all gone," Fabiana said, almost spitting. "You took everything."

She let loose a spate of curses in rapid Italian and pounced again, this time straight at Tamar's chest.

Tamar parried with the purse, heard the blade crush into the straw, felt the force against her body, felt the prick of the dagger embed in the purse.

The purse dropped over the railing, tumbled purse over dagger, dagger over purse onto the stone floor of the foyer.

"*Merda*," Fabiana said and grabbed Tamar's injured arm, wrenched it.

The pain flared up into her shoulder.

Footsteps in the foyer, Ercole shouting, "No, no, no."

Fabiana clutched Tamar's sleeve. The sleeve tore away.

"No, no, no," from down below. Fabiana looked down.

Tamar pushed her back, back, scrambled out from behind the desk and Fabiana charged, rammed with her head.

Tamar staggered, lost her balance, backed farther, fell to the floor, her back against the stand of the Kore.

She saw it rock, tilt off the plinth. She closed her eyes, crossed her arms over her head, ducked and rolled away.

She heard a thump, heard a groan from Fabiana, heard the Kore shatter.

"No, no, no."

She opened her eyes, saw Fabiana on the floor, still gripping Tamar's torn sleeve, her eyes still open, her head at an odd angle. The broken Kore lay smashed on the floor next to her head.

Ercole had come up the stairs, bent over Fabiana and let out a soft cry. He sat on the floor with Fabiana's head in his arms and rocked back and forth.

"Is she breathing?" Tamar asked and sat down next to him. She couldn't stop shaking.

Still rocking, Ercole leaned down, listened with his head close to Fabiana's face. Tears ran down, over the bridge of his nose, across his cheek, onto Fabiana's open eyes, and he continued rocking.

"Does she have a pulse?" Tamar asked.

Ercole's nose was running. He wiped it with the back of his hand, fumbled for Fabiana's wrist, and began to sob.

Tamar started to reach out to him, then changed her mind.

She crept down the stairs. Her hand, sticky and wet with blood, clutched the banister.

She searched in her pocket for the card Fischer had given her, went into the small alcove off the living room, and called him.

She sat in the alcove, staring out the window until she saw Fischer's car pull up and went to the door to let him in. Enzio was with him.

Enzio looked at the cut on her arm, her torn, bloodstained dress. "You certainly are hard on your clothes," he said.

She led them up to the gallery. Fischer knelt down next to Fabiana, felt for a pulse, then shook his head. He looked over at Ercole, seated on the bottom step of the stairway, his hands pressed against his forehead.

"My name is Benito Motti," he said. "I come from Cortina."

Chapter Thirty

Lyon, France, August 22, 1990

They had just finished lunch at an outdoor café overlooking the Rhône and drunk a half a bottle of Beaujolais. The breeze coming off the river was bright with the first hint of autumn and dried leaves swirled in little eddies on the pavement around the table.

Tamar sat back and closed her eyes while the sharp autumn air fanned her hair.

Enzio lit a cigarette. The smell was sharp, acrid, and somehow familiar.

"Different brand?" Tamar asked, her eyes still closed.

"Turkish."

The smell of the cigarette combined with the gentle wind off the river tugged at her memory.

"You should really give up smoking," she said.

There was a crisp day just like this one, she remembered. There was a small stucco house with a sign that said "The Future Foretold, Palms Read" that hung from the porch and swung in an autumn breeze.

"She's very good," her grandmother had said as they drove down Whittier Boulevard. "She's never wrong."

"Did she tell you about the accident?" Tamar asked, about the day everything changed.

"Don't be impertinent." Her grandmother had narrowed her eyes. "She warned me that someday I would be burdened with the upbringing of an impudent child."

That was supposed to be enough to keep her quiet, but Tamar said, "Can she read my fortune too?"

"You're only a child," her grandmother said, as if her future would not be fully formed until after voting age.

"I'm thirteen. If I were in Samoa, I would be married, with children. Margaret Mead says so."

"You're wrong," her grandmother said.

Inside, the house of the fortune-teller smelled of cigarettes and damp, mice and stale cookies. The fortune-teller had long earrings and a scarf on her head, and her fingers seemed to curl and cup around her words when she spoke. Her name was Zelika.

Tamar sat in a chair against the wall while Zelika scanned her grandmother's hand and told her grandmother what she wanted to hear.

And then, Zelika looked over at Tamar. "For the young lady, I have something special," she said.

Her grandmother was about to remonstrate, but Zelika had already gone through the curtain into the back of the house. She returned a few minutes later with a bowl of ice water and a saucepan she clutched with a padded glove at arm's length.

"No charge," she said.

She put the bowl on the table. The contents of the saucepan hit the water in the bowl with a sizzle.

"Melted lead," she said.

Tamar came over to the table and saw a shiny tangle of bones and skulls at the bottom of the bowl.

"You're going to marry a doctor," her grandmother declared.

"She's going to marry, but the marriage will end in tragedy."

Her grandmother gave her another accusatory look, as if to say she brings on all this tragedy herself. Maybe she was right. Years later in the Yucatan, when Tamar gazed at reliefs along the base of a ball court with the bones and skulls like the lead drippings, she remembered her grandmother.

"But she will find another," Zelika continued.

Her grandmother looked skeptical. "She will?"

"Someone who deceives her when they meet," Zelika said, and Tamar felt a chill of apprehension and longed for safety.

"You do séances?" Tamar asked.

Her grandmother yanked at her arm and gave her a look that would freeze a penguin.

But Zelika bent down and stroked her cheek.

"I can't bring back your momma and poppa, little one," she said. "No one can bring back the dead."

"What are you thinking?" Enzio asked. "You look like you're asleep."

She opened her eyes and sat straight in the chair. "No. Just thinking."

"About Gilberto?"

She contemplated the water. An excursion boat passed, going downriver.

"Sort of," she said. "Gilberto, Mustafa, Chatham, Orman, the whole thing. That first day I was at Gilberto's, when Fabiana gave the deposition to the police about the coins Firenzano stole when she left the basement window open, Gilberto was angry that they let Firenzano go."

"Gilberto was angry about the whole thing—that Fabiana had set it up. She used the coins to pay Firenzano. It didn't cost them anything. Fabiana figured that Firenzano would be released as soon as she gave the deposition to the police, and the insurance would pay for the coins when Gilberto reported the theft to the police."

Tamar nodded, said, "Hmm," and played with her napkin. "I still don't understand why Chatham was killed."

"Chatham and Mustafa were partners, and Fabiana was on to them."

"The fresco that never arrived?"

He nodded. "That and other things. It was dangerous to cross Fabiana. They were cheating her."

"But why?"

"Chatham needed money. He hated his wife, but needed his own money to get away from her."

"So Firenzano followed Chatham from Turkey on the train and killed Chatham on orders from Fabiana. And Demitrius and Irena were in on it."

"No, they had a different scam going. Chatham fell for it. Finding the Thracian gold was a windfall for Firenzano."

"But why Chatham? Why not Mustafa? Mustafa was the one in Basel."

"He was supposed to be next. Fabiana was waiting for Firenzano to get back from The Hague."

"Where he killed Orman."

"Fabiana didn't plan that. He killed Orman on his own. After he got the money from the Thracian gold, he got more independent, didn't just take orders from Fabiana. Besides, Orman was getting too close."

Enzio lifted the bottle of Beaujolais and was about to pour some into her glass.

She put her hand over the rim. "No more for me, thanks. I'll fall asleep during the interview."

"Gives you courage."

"I'll have to find courage on my own."

He shrugged and reached for the bottle of Evian water to pour into her glass.

"And Mustafa? Why did he need money?"

"His money was going to Freedom Fighters for Kurdistan. Mustafa is a bit of an idealist."

"He did it for the Yezidi?"

"No. The Yezidi are peace loving. These are Kurdish extremists fighting for an independent Kurdistan, Kurds from Turkey, Syria, and Iraq."

"What about the Aristides?" Tamar asked. "Were they in on it?"

"Not at all. Leandro is busy working on his corpus of Byzantine coins and Madame Aristides is in Paris for her annual session with her plastic surgeon."

"I think Mustafa liked the irony of financing rebels with antiquities stolen from Turkey," Tamar said. "He cheated Fabiana because he probably thought she deserved to be cheated."

"He blamed Gilberto. That's why he killed him."

"For Chatham's death?" She grasped the stem of the glass and twirled it. "I don't think Gilberto knew the full extent of what Fabiana was doing," she said.

Enzio nodded "Gilberto was an easy dupe. He was too busy enjoying his sybaritic life-style—cases of the best vintages automatically sent over by the wine merchant, epicurean lunches with the elite—the prince of antiquity dealers. Fabiana manipulated him."

Tamar sighed and took a sip of water. "He knew what was going on." She watched the white caps on the river rise and fall, whipped by tiny gusts of autumn breeze. "He let Fabiana take care of the dirty work."

They both fell silent, gazing at the boats that moved dreamily along the river, at the gentle motion of the current, listening to the water slip back and forth along the riverbank.

"Will you be going back to Hazarfen next season?"

"After all that's happened?"

"You found what you came after in Basel," he said.

"I found the mosaic, if that's what you mean."

"And you broke up an illegal antiquities operation."

"I suppose." She looked at the river, not at Enzio. "It's all gone now. Benito will sell off what's left and go back to Cortina."

"Not really," he said. "He's now Ercole Sforza, the CEO of Sforza Galleries."

"Sforza Galleries?"

"With branches in Paris, New York, and Berlin. He's developed a new wrinkle for the antiquities trade. He's selling franchises. He provides the design for displays, sets up the galleries, then sells them overpriced antiquities that have been artfully mounted on acrylic bases and gives them letters of authenticity and provenance. He seems to have an endless supply."

"So that's what happened to the Roman Kybele. All the antiquities come from the collection of the Marquis de Cuvier?"

"No, some come from the family collection of the descendants of Baron Von Humboldt."

"Humboldt was a nineteenth-century geologist."

"Who would be in a better position to collect antiquities?"

"He never married. He didn't have descendants."

"That's the beauty of it."

"Did anyone find the Kybele missing from Ephesus?" Tamar asked.

"Not yet. Rome wasn't sacked in a day." He leaned back. "Besides, it was on loan from a certain Demitrius Konstantinopoulis."

"Mustafa was casing Ephesus, you know. He was checking out the security in the museum."

"I wouldn't doubt it." Enzio signaled the waiter.

"*L'addition*," he said and stood up.

"We have to go or you'll be late," he told Tamar. "Have to find a taxi."

He totaled up the check again when the waiter brought it, running his finger quickly down the edge of the paper, left a pile of franc notes and took what was left of the Evian water.

◇◇◇

The taxi left them off near the gate.

Tamar gaped at the high green iron fence topped with razor wire, at the reflecting pool around the concrete and glass building.

"Your mother's house?" Tamar asked.

Enzio nodded. "As the French would say, *Formidable*."

The gendarmes at the gate inspected her passport and waved her on toward an intercom at the front gate.

"Nothing to be afraid of," Enzio said.

"I'm not afraid," she said, and realized that for the first time in a long time she wasn't afraid at all.

To receive a free catalog of Poisoned Pen Press titles, please contact us in one of the following ways:

Phone: 1-800-421-3976
Facsimile: 1-480-949-1707
E-mail: info@poisonedpenpress.com
Website: www.poisonedpenpress.com

Poisoned Pen Press
6962 E. First Ave. Ste. 103
Scottsdale, AZ 85251